Also by John D. Nesbitt
in Large Print:

Wild Rose of Ruby Canyon
Black Diamond Rendezvous
One-Eyed Cowboy Wild
One Foot in the Stirrup
Twin Rivers

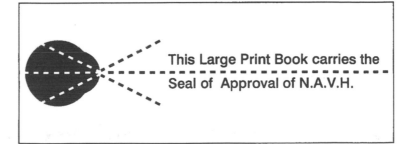

This Large Print Book carries the
Seal of Approval of N.A.V.H.

Man from
Wolf River

Man from Wolf River

John D. Nesbitt

G.K. Hall & Co. • Waterville, Maine

Published in 2002 by arrangement with Leisure Books,
a division of Dorchester Publishing Co., Inc.

G.K. Hall Large Print Western Series.

The text of this Large Print edition is unabridged.
Other aspects of the book may vary from the original edition.

Set in 16 pt. Plantin by Myrna S. Raven.

Printed in the United States on permanent paper.

Library of Congress Cataloging-in-Publication Data

Nesbitt, John D.
    Man from Wolf River / John D. Nesbitt.
      p. cm.
    ISBN 0-7838-9744-8 (lg. print : hc : alk. paper)
    1. Wyoming — Fiction.   2. Large type books. I. Title.
PS3564.E76 M36 2002
  813'.54—dc21   2001051774

For Wayne Deahl

Chapter One

The man from Wolf River sat straight in the saddle as he drank a mug of cold beer in the doorway of the Blue Horse Saloon. Riders up and down the trail said it was something a fellow ought to try if he went through Cameron, Wyoming. They said the proprietor didn't mind, especially if the rider tipped a dime or two bits. So Owen Felver gave it a try. He had gotten the chestnut horse to step up onto the board sidewalk and partway into the saloon, and now the horse stood relaxed with its head forward as Felver drank the cold beer and enjoyed it.

When he had finished the beer and handed the mug back to the barkeep, along with a tip, he backed the horse out through the doorway and turned it on the board sidewalk. It took a little spurring to get the horse to step back down into the street, but Felver managed it. Once in the street, he turned the horse around and nudged it up to the hitching rail where he had tied his brown packhorse a while earlier. As he dismounted and tied the saddle horse to the rail, he became aware of two men off to his left.

One man was bent toward the window of a café, shading his eyes and looking in. The other man was sitting on a bench against the wall of the café. He sat in the shadow of the man who was standing, but he looked familiar. With a quick thought, Felver recalled seeing the man on the bench earlier. He had been sitting and watching as Felver urged the chestnut horse up onto the sidewalk and into the doorway of the saloon.

As Felver stepped onto the sidewalk and paused, facing the man, he heard one of them speak.

"I don't see her in here."

It was the man at the window who spoke. Even from the back, Felver could tell that he was well dressed. He looked like a businessman, with a dark brown suit and a narrow-brimmed hat to match.

"Here she comes now," said the man on the bench, motioning with his head to his left.

The man at the window straightened up and turned. He was slender and a couple of inches taller than average. His hat brim cast a shadow on a pair of deep brown eyes that were set close together. He had a dark Vandyke beard and dark hair, and he carried himself with an air of importance.

Felver looked down the sidewalk to his right, in the direction where the two men were looking. He saw a young woman coming their way. She was wearing a gray cotton dress, light and loose for summer wear, but she looked shapely enough to hold his interest. Her light-colored hair reached her

8

shoulders and swayed as she walked.

Felver glanced back at the two men. The tall man had drawn himself up straight in a pose that expressed authority. He wore a clean, close-necked white shirt, a dark tie, and a buttoned dark brown vest that matched the rest of his suit. Across the vest lay a gold watch chain, glinting in the afternoon sun. The man looked to be in his mid-forties.

The man on the bench leaned forward, out of the shadow, and looked in the direction of the approaching woman. Felver could see he was a younger man, maybe in his mid-twenties. He wore a bowler hat and a light brown suit, lighter than the other man's and not so neat. He wore a pale white shirt, open at the neck, and his watch chain hung forward as he leaned to see the woman.

Felver glanced back at the young woman, who was within a dozen yards now. Her face had an expression of dislike, which seemed to be directed at the tall man.

"I've been looking for you," said the man in the neat suit.

"You don't need to," she answered. Slowing to a stop, she gave him a hard look and said, "I told you I don't want anything from you. Now, if you'll excuse me, I want to go in here." She nodded in the direction of the café door, which the man in the spade beard had partly blocked off.

The man didn't move. "You ought to use a

little more sense," he said, "and not be running up and down the street like a little —"

The man held his tongue as the girl looked at Felver. It was as if the man didn't realize someone else had been watching.

Felver could tell that something was not right. As a general rule he liked to mind his own business, but he sensed that the girl needed help and the man in the suit didn't have any claim on her.

Felver met her glance. She had light blue eyes, nicely shaped facial features, and a faint tan on her face. She looked troubled, but she also had a plain, working-class air about her that said it wasn't the first trouble she had seen.

He looked at the man with the close-set eyes and said, "Why don't you let her by, like she asked?"

The taller man gave him a cold look, as if he was used to giving orders and not taking them, and said, "Why don't you stay out of it?"

Felver arched his eyebrows and turned back to look at the girl. He noticed her pretty chin and mouth before he met her eyes again. He saw the same look as before, a look that said she could use help.

"Is this man anything to you?" he asked.

The girl glanced at the other man and back at Felver. "No."

Felver looked back at the man in the neat suit. "It seems to me that you're the one that could stay out of other people's business. Why don't you quit lookin' in windows and blockin' doorways, and let this young lady walk by?"

The man with the close-set eyes flinched, and Felver thought he caught a flicker of something pass between the man standing and the man sitting, even though they didn't look at each other. Maybe the fellow didn't like being taken down a notch in front of other people. Whatever he didn't like, it was making his face and neck turn red.

An answer came. "Wherever you're from, it seems as if they don't teach young pups to watch what they say." As he spoke, he moved a short step to his right, almost directly in front of the young man on the bench, who sank back into the shadow. The path was open to the doorway, but the girl stood still.

"I come from a place called Heedon, up on the Wolf River, if it's anything to you. My name's Owen Felver, and I stand behind whatever I say."

The other man gave a lift to his chin. "My name's Henry Coper, if it's anything to you, and I'll just say that a smart boy like you belongs back in South Dakota, stacking wheat."

Felver smiled. If there was one thing he didn't expect to be caught doing, it was stacking wheat. He put his thumbs in his belt and said, "I go where I want, Mr. Coper."

The taller man nodded. "You do that." He turned to the girl, touched his hat brim, and

11

said, "Miss Quoin." Then he turned to his right and walked away.

Felver looked at the girl and nodded. He could feel a smile on his face.

"Thank you, Mr. Felver," she said, holding out her hand. "I'm Jenny Quoin, and I appreciate your help."

"Glad to be useful," he said, still smiling as he reached for her hand. "You can just call me Owen." He motioned with his head in the direction where Coper had gone. "After all, I'm just a boy."

She laughed. "And I'm just a girl. You can call me Jenny."

"Good enough," he said as their hands separated. He took a quick look at her and imagined she was probably in her early twenties — a girl in some senses of the word. "I hope to see you again."

"Yes, I hope so." The trouble was gone from her face, and her light blue eyes had a soft shine. She looked at the young man on the bench, then at the door of the café, and back at Felver. "Well, excuse me, then. I was on my way inside."

Felver, who did not sense that he was being invited, tipped his hat and said, "Go ahead. We'll see you later." As he watched her walk away, he thought she really was rather nice-looking for a working girl.

He turned to look at the man on the bench, who had taken out a curved-stem pipe and was stuffing it with tobacco. Felver saw, as before, that the man was young — probably a year or two younger than Felver himself. He saw now that the man had brown eyes, brown hair, and a full mustache. Felver thought the young man was drawing out a dramatic moment, for he struck something of a somber pose as he loaded his pipe and then lit it.

"Friend of yours?" asked Felver, with a nod in the direction that Coper had taken.

The young man shook his head as he blew out a cloud of smoke. "Not so much."

"Name's Felver, as you might have heard."

The young man's mustache twitched as he settled the pipe stem in his mouth. He made a grave nod and said, "Name's Tom. Tom Heid." He raised his right hand to cup his pipe, then puffed out two quick clouds of smoke.

Seeing that there wouldn't be a handshake, Felver hooked his thumbs in his belt again. "Pleased to meet you."

"Likewise." The young man twitched his nose, and the mustache went up and down. "Ridin' through?"

Felver glanced at the café door where he had seen the girl walk through. "Not in any hurry."

Heid shifted his pipe and said, "No need to be."

From the smugness of the tone, Felver couldn't tell whether Heid was implying that Coper was harmless or that Jenny Quoin was attractive. Maybe he meant both.

Felver said, "Uh-huh." Taking another look at Heid, he wondered what the young man did for work. He was dressed like a storekeeper, but he wasn't very well scrubbed, and he didn't seem to be in a hurry to get back to a sales counter and cash box. He looked as if he was of average height and build, but he wasn't husky or muscular. The hands that fiddled with the pipe looked soft; they certainly had not had much contact with a pitchfork or shovel.

Felver wondered how men like Coper and Heid could wear a full suit in the middle of summer. Maybe they didn't move around very much, so their fire didn't burn very hot. It made him uncomfortable just to see a man dressed that way in warm weather, unless he was a preacher.

"Warmin' up," he said.

Heid nodded with the pipe in his mouth. "Yeah, but it's a dry heat."

Felver looked up at the sun. He had originally planned to go in and drink another beer, but he thought better of it now. "Well, I think I'll take these two horses to get a drink of water."

Heid said something that was hard to catch. It sounded like "Thing to do."

"Nice meetin' you," Felver said as he moved to the edge of the sidewalk.

"My pleasure."

Felver glanced at the café window to see if he could catch a glimpse of the girl Jenny, but all

14

he saw was a reflection of the bright glare of the street. As he turned away, he realized he had also seen the darker reflection of Heid's head and shoulders.

At the livery stable where he watered the horses, Felver asked about the country west of town. The stable man told him that if he followed Red Creek upstream about a mile or so, he would come to a good camping spot at Red Bluff. Felver thanked him and rode out of town.

At the Red Bluff campsite, Felver could see where other people had camped in a grove of cottonwoods on the north side of the creek and a little downstream from the bluff, which lay on the south side of a curve in the creek. Felver chose a spot beyond the cottonwoods, just opposite the bluff. He figured he was trading shade for better grass. A clump of chokecherry bushes on the west side of his camp would give late-afternoon shade, and it looked like a decent windbreak. The chokecherry bushes had grown to a height of ten or twelve feet, so even if they didn't give midday shade, they would not drop any big, dead branches in a high wind.

He unsaddled one horse and unloaded the other, then set them both out on pickets to graze. Next he took off his boots and socks and crossed the creek, ax in hand, to cut down a couple of cottonwood saplings. He carried them back across on his shoulder and laid them

15

at the spot where he expected to pitch his tent. Then he sat in the sun for a few minutes to let his feet dry. Making camp in good weather was always a pleasure. Everything was new — to him, at least — and a little bit of work made a good camp. The light breeze felt cool on his clean toes, and he enjoyed these few minutes of necessary loafing.

He thought of the girl, Jenny. She was a nice-looking one, all right. He wondered what the story was on her, and he wondered how hard it would be to find her if he went back into town.

When he had his boots back on, he unpacked his camp. He rolled out his tent east and west, with the flap facing east. He pegged out the bottom, raised the ridge with the poles he had cut, and stretched out the sides with guy ropes. It was a good tent — six by ten, with three-foot walls and a five-foot ridge. He could move around all right inside, for as much as a fellow needed to do inside a tent.

He gathered rocks and set a fire pit about five yards from the flap of his tent. Then with the ax he went upstream a quarter of a mile, where he found some deadfall. He cut up enough wood for an evening and then a morning fire, and in two trips he had it all back in camp.

The shade of the chokecherry trees was starting to touch the tent, and he thought of the girl again. It wasn't that long of a ride back into town, so even if he didn't find her, he wouldn't be out much. He gathered up the chestnut horse, watered and saddled him, and headed back to town.

He went first to the café, where he had last seen her. He half expected to see Heid still sitting in front, but the bench was empty. Felver tied his horse to the rail, stepped up onto the sidewalk, and walked to the door without peeking in through the window first.

Once inside, he did not see the girl. It was a little darker inside than it was outside, and a light haze of smoke hung in the air. He could smell fried food and coffee as well as tobacco smoke. Men sat at a couple of tables, and no one paid him much attention as he closed the door behind him.

Then he saw the girl Jenny. She was coming out of the kitchen with a plate of food in each hand. He caught her eye as she walked toward him. They exchanged smiles, and she turned to set the plates down at a table. Felver moved to the opposite side of the café and took a seat by himself.

In a little while she came by and asked what he would like. He said he would start with coffee.

When she brought the cup of coffee, he thought it would be just as well to eat supper, so he ordered a plate of steak and potatoes. He had liked the looks of the two plates she had set down at the other table, and the pleasant smell of food encouraged him.

She paused after taking his order. "I want to

thank you again for helping me this afternoon."

"Quite all right. I didn't mind it."

"I was on my way to work here for the first time, and I didn't want any trouble."

"Oh. Uh-huh." Felver was tempted to ask what trouble there might have been, but he couldn't think of a question that wasn't too inquisitive.

She must have felt there was a need for some sort of explanation, for she said, in a low voice, "There's a bit of a story behind it, and I wouldn't mind telling you. I feel like I owe you that much, but this isn't a very good place." She motioned with her head toward the other customers.

"Sure," he said. "We can talk later. Anytime."

She nodded and smiled and then walked back to the kitchen.

Felver sipped his coffee and enjoyed it. He appreciated the leisure of sitting at a table and drinking coffee out of a crockery mug. He had drunk plenty of coffee out of hot tin cups, often in a hurry as he crouched in a cow camp, so he enjoyed a good moment when he could have it. Besides, he had never seen a girl like this at any cow camp or bunkhouse.

When she came with his plate of food, she set it down in front of him with a knife and a fork. While she was still near him, she asked, "Do you live around here?"

"No, not for long, anyway. As you probably gathered from that earlier conversation, I'm on my way through. But I did find a pretty good camping spot out of town a little ways, so I'll be around long enough to have a chat."

"Where's your camp?"

"About a mile or so out of town, right on the creek. They call it Red Creek, and I'm camped right across from a bluff they call Red Bluff."

"That's not too far. I could walk there if I felt like it."

He smiled at her. "You're not afraid?"

She smiled. "Not in the daytime. I could walk out there in the morning. I don't go to work here until noon."

"That would be all right," he said. "I'll stick around camp in the morning — not that I have anywhere to go, anyway."

Felver ate his fried steak and potatoes. The steak was a little dry, but he washed it down with coffee. He took his time eating, and the café began to fill up. The customers were all men, most of them in hats and boots. Felver did not recognize any of them, and none of them paid much attention to him.

A bald-headed fat man came in to sit at the cash box. He lit a cigar and settled into his chair with the air of a proprietor. Felver guessed he was.

Jenny stayed busy with her other customers, so Felver didn't get a chance to speak with her again except for a thank-you when she brought coffee. When he got up to pay for his meal, she was in the kitchen, so he paid the man at the cash box and went out into the cool evening.

He found his way back to camp in the dark without any trouble. The packhorse was still grazing on his picket, and the camp was just as he had left it. He built a fire to chase away the dark for a little while. Opening the flap of his tent to let in the light, he went inside and rolled out his bed, which still carried some of the afternoon warmth. He dug into his war bag and took out a coat, which he folded and put in place for a pillow. The inside of the tent seemed cozy, with its familiar objects and smells.

Felver lay down on his bed and clasped his hands behind his head. Beyond the open flap of the tent, small flames danced in the fire pit. It wouldn't hurt to lay over an extra day, he thought.

Fielding had told him the work didn't get started until the first of July, or at least he wouldn't need another hand until then. Fielding was a packer, and he hauled grub and supplies to the cow camps and sheep camps up in the mountains. As the camps moved up higher with the onset of summer, he would need another man. They had struck a deal by which Felver could work spring roundup on the Wolf River and then work for summer wages with Fielding in the Laramie Mountains. It seemed like a good prospect — a man would get to see new country, and he could pick up a little knowledge about packs and diamond hitches and such knots as might come in handy someday. He could load his own packhorse just fine, but loading a string of mules with who knows what and taking them over a mountain trail — well, that would be a higher level of accomplishment.

Felver thought about the time and season. The Fourth of July had already slipped by, what with the end of spring roundup and a few days' travel. But Fielding had said to come when roundup was through, and he had done that. It was still early summer in the high country, for all that it was hot and dry down here. A day's layover shouldn't make that much difference.

Chapter Two

Felver awoke in the calm of morning. He started a new fire with the coals left over from the night before. The firewood was holding out fine. He went to the creek for water, and while he was at it he washed his face. The cool water made him feel fresh and clean. Back at the camp he made coffee and set the pot on a rock at the edge of the fire. Then he went for the horses. After he took them to the creek for water, he decided to picket them a little farther out. It was a fine morning, cool and fresh in the early daylight. The horses had rested well and seemed brimming with energy as he took them out to better grass.

On his way back to camp, he saw that the girl Jenny had arrived. The sun hadn't yet cleared the cottonwoods, so she must have gotten an early start. She was standing a few yards away from the fire pit, and he could see she was wearing the same gray dress she had worn the day before. As they waved to each other, he was glad he had washed his face earlier.

When he was within speaking distance he said, "Looks like you decided to walk in the cool of morning."

"It's just as well. And besides, there's not so many people up and about."

"Well, it's a nice morning, and I think the coffee's just about ready." He looked around the campsite, wondering where she might sit. "I've got some canvas packs in the tent," he said. "That could give you a cushion to sit on."

"Thanks," she said.

Jenny took a seat on the folded canvas as Felver poured the coffee. He took a seat on the ground near her, and for a moment they sipped coffee without talking. Again, he liked her looks — she was a little common in her general appearance, but she had pretty facial features and an appealing figure.

"You found a nice place to put your camp," she said.

"Uh-huh. It's worth remembering in case a fellow ever comes back this way." He looked at her and then glanced around the campsite. As a matter of habit he looked off to his left and checked his horses, then scanned the rest of the area. Something out of place caught his eye — something in the shade of the cottonwood grove.

"Do you see something?" she asked.

He could make out shapes now. "Did you bring someone with you?"

"No, why?"

"It looks like two men on horses over there in the cottonwoods." He looked at her. "Do you think someone followed you?"

Her eyebrows went up. "I don't know. They could have."

Felver twisted his mouth. "Well, I guess I should wave 'em on in. I don't like the idea of them sittin' over there and gawkin' at us."

He looked at her again and she nodded, so he stood up and walked out to the edge of his camp. He waved at the men on horseback, and as they moved out of the trees he could see he did not know either of them. The only men he knew around here were Coper and Heid, and these two were a different breed of pup. For one thing, they both wore riding and working clothes. The one on his left was also too heavy to be either Coper or Heid.

The sun was clearing the cottonwoods now, and Felver didn't like the idea of looking at these fellows with the sun in his eyes. As he walked back to Jenny, he decided he would wait till they rode in and then he would walk around and face them from the north.

"Do you know them?" he asked as the riders came nearer.

"I'm not sure. I think I saw them last night. They look like a couple of smart ones who came in to eat."

"Well, we'll see what they want."

The riders called out a greeting from about forty yards, and Felver called them in. When they came to a stop, he walked around to the north as he had planned, and the riders shifted their horses to face him.

"What can I do for you gents?" he called out.

24

"It looked like this girl got lost," said the one on the right.

Felver looked at the rider. He was a youngster, hardly twenty years old, wearing a tied-down six-gun. He wore black, knee-high boots with the trousers tucked in, and he also wore leather wrist cuffs, which might not help him draw his pistol but might look fashionable in a saloon. He also wore a vest, and a shirt that looked clean. Felver decided he looked like a well-dressed saddle tramp.

"I don't think she's lost if she's in my camp."

"She was supposed to meet us," said the other rider.

"Is that right?" Felver turned his gaze at the heavyset rider, who wore no vest, only a shirt that spilled over his belt. This one was young too, but not as dapper as his partner. He had thick lips and droopy eyes, and he seemed to sag in the saddle. He had a gun on his hip too, and it gave Felver a clear sense of where his own gun was — right next to the head of his bedroll.

"Yes, it is," said the first rider. "She was supposed to give us something."

Felver could feel himself getting mad, but he got hold of himself. These two looked like a couple of troublemakers, and they might try to goad him into a fight. They had probably followed the girl out of town like a couple of dogs with their tongues hanging out. He could imagine their thinking she was available, and he decided to lay things out straight and not let them talk in their innuendoes any more.

He turned to the girl. "Do you have anything for these two?"

Her face was clear and her voice was steady. "No, I don't know what they're talking about. I didn't say anything to them except what it took to serve them a meal."

Felver turned back to look at the two riders. Both of them had their hands up on their saddle horns, in clear sight. "There must be a mistake," he said. "You heard the lady."

"Maybe it's your mistake," said the heavyset rider.

Felver's answer came quickly. "Look here. I don't know who you fellows are, but let's keep it civil. There's a lady present, and this is my camp, and I suggest you not say anything that a man shouldn't say."

That stopped them for a minute. Felver could feel their hesitation. Anyone who even thought he was a man would know better than to insult a woman in public. Even speaking a nice girl's name in a saloon was enough to earn a black eye. Maybe Jenny wasn't a nice girl, but if either of these fellows crossed the line and called her a liar or a trollop, they would bring on trouble that could go beyond this camp. Calling them on it in front of someone else had taken some of the wind out of them.

Felver spoke again. "Since this is my camp, I think I've got a right to ask you your names. Mine's Felver."

He looked at the heavyset rider with droopy eyes. The thick lips moved.

"My name's Hodges."

"And mine's Carter."

Felver looked at the rider with the high boots, who brought his horse a couple of steps closer and looked down. Felver had the urge to pull him off his horse and trounce him, but a calm thought prevailed.

"Well," he said, "now that we got that part taken care of, I could ask if there was anything else on your mind."

"Just one thing," said Carter without much delay.

Felver looked up at him. "What's that?"

Carter tilted his head toward the camp. "You ought to pull your stakes and roll up your camp while the gettin's good."

Felver looked again at the man and wondered how a decent-looking young fellow could have turned into an upstart troublemaker.

"Don't worry about me or my camp," he said. "I won't pull my stakes until I feel like it." He glanced at the girl and back at the riders. "Now, if you'll excuse us, we were having a conversation."

"Looks like it," said Hodges, turning his horse.

Carter said nothing more. He just looked down at Jenny with a sneer and spurred his horse, turning it and kicking up a cloud of dust.

Felver watched the two riders as the horses pounded away. "Good riddance," he said. He turned to the girl and smiled. "Now, what do you say about something for breakfast? I've got some bacon and cold biscuits, if you don't mind that."

She smiled. "It sounds fine."

Felver went into the tent and dug through his bag of provisions, where he found the bacon wrapped in a cloth. Back at the fire he unwrapped the chunk of bacon and took out his pocketknife. The girl hadn't said anything for several minutes, and now she spoke.

"I came here to work for Mr. Coper."

Felver looked up from slicing bacon. "Oh." After a moment's thought he spoke again. "What sort of business does he have?"

"He's got a business called Five Star Drayage."

"Oh, a shipping business."

"Yes. But I didn't go to work for him there. I went to work at his house."

"Oh." Felver kept himself from asking anything, and the silence hung for a second.

"Yes. I was to be his housekeeper, or hired girl. He had had others."

"Uh-huh."

"Do you know his wife?"

Felver shrugged. "I didn't know he had one. I barely know him. That was the only time I had anything to do with him, when you were there."

Jenny nodded. "He has a wife — a nice lady,

as far as that goes. But she's very fat. She can't do very much of the housework, so he's had hired girls. One after another, I guess."

"Do they have children?"

"Do you mean Mr. and Mrs. Coper? No, but I don't think she's always been that fat. It's something that happened to her after they were married."

"Sort of a condition, then."

"Yes, something that came upon her."

Felver set the bacon to sizzle in the skillet, which he had laid on the coals. "So he runs off all the hired girls, uh?"

"That's what it seems like. Of course, there weren't any around for me to ask."

"I guess."

"Anyway, as it turned out, once I got there, it seemed like he wanted a chamber maid and not just a hired girl to sweep the floors and do the wash."

Felver poked at the bacon with his knife. "From meetin' him, I could imagine him bein' that type."

The girl was silent for a moment and then spoke. "He always made me feel uncomfortable. I didn't like the way he looked at me."

Felver made himself look her in the eyes as he said, "Uh-huh."

"Maybe it was just me, but I felt as if he was looking at me even when I was in my room."

Felver imagined Coper at the keyhole. "I could see where he'd give someone that feelin'."

"Well, I just couldn't stand it anymore. It seemed like his wife had some idea of what he was up to but couldn't do anything about it. He seemed to show up in every room I was in, and it wasn't too long before the whole house gave me the jimjams. So after a week, I moved out and got a room at the hotel. Then after a couple more days I got a job at the café."

"That's where I came in."

"Yes. He had been trying to get me to go back, and I think he was making one more try."

"Well, he didn't do a very good job of it."

"No, and I'll be damned if I'd ever go back. I'm sure he has a peephole somewhere, but I didn't find it, and I wasn't going to stay around and look for it. I 'bout like to die of the creeps as it was."

As Felver heard the girl speak, he formed a stronger sense of what he had thought before. She wasn't very squeamish about how she spoke or what she spoke of. In spite of her nice looks, she must have come from a working-class background or lower. She had a casual air about her, too, but even at that she seemed honest.

He looked at her as he spoke. "If you don't mind my askin', how did you come to meet him?"

"I was in Cheyenne. I was . . . stranded there, and I needed to earn some wages."

"Oh. I didn't mean to pry."

"No, that's all right. I might as well tell you

sooner than later."

Felver turned to the skillet and flipped over the four slices of bacon. They had browned well on the underside. He looked back at Jenny. "Go ahead," he said. "It won't go any farther than this camp."

She hesitated, then took a deep breath and let it out. "I don't think I was a bad girl," she said. "Just not a smart one. I wanted to get out of the house, so I ran off with a man. We were going to get married. We got as far as Cheyenne, and he left me there. He just up and left without a word, and there I was without a cent."

"Sounds kinda tough."

"Well, it was. But I can't say it wasn't my fault." She seemed to reflect for a second before she spoke again. "I probably looked like easy pickin's to Mr. Coper."

"Well, at least you've got a job of your own now." Felver looked at her, and he could see she still had her pride.

"Yes, I do," she said, almost with defiance. "And I don't know what makes men think they can just follow a girl out of town."

Felver recalled the image of Hodges and Carter. "Those boys'll just get themselves in trouble, that's what. They get their pot a-boilin' with too low a heat."

"Well," she said, giving Felver a square look, "I didn't give them any encouragement. I'll say that."

He looked at her and smiled. "I wouldn't

have thought you did."

Her face relaxed into a smile. "Thanks."

"It's all right," he said, lifting a slice of brown bacon. "It looks like we've got this cooked. I'll go into the tent and get those cold biscuits I spoke of, and I believe it's breakfast."

When the morning meal was over and the sun climbed a little higher in the sky, Jenny said she needed to get back to town. Felver offered to let her ride one of his horses, but she said her dress wouldn't allow it. She said she would just as soon walk, so Felver decided to walk with her and lead his horse.

Once in town, she thanked him again for all his help and for his hospitality. They touched hands, and then she was gone into the hotel.

On his way back out of town, Felver wondered which house was Coper's. Behind the walls of one of them, he imagined, was the place where girls had lived in fear with a prowling master and his helpless wife. That sort of thing had always seemed to belong in the cities, he thought, but now he could imagine it was just a matter of where a fellow like Coper happened to end up.

Out of town and under the open sky, he thought of Jenny. He liked her well enough, but he wasn't sure if he liked her the way he was supposed to like a nice girl or if he liked her for the possibilities suggested by the shapely figure beneath the gray cotton dress. She was a fallen woman, and a man could sense that, but she had her dignity, too. Maybe he liked her in the right way, even if he liked her in the other way, too. He had treated her with respect in both of the little run-ins he had had, and he felt good about that.

As he rode on, another awareness began to creep upon him. Between the two incidents he felt he had almost made something of a declaration, like he was taking up her cause and wanted her to be his woman, or something. He could imagine other men — like Heid — smirking at the idea of being gallant with someone else's leavings. Well, to hell with them. As far as things went between him and her, which wasn't very far, he thought she was all right.

As he thought about it all, he couldn't shake the image he had of Hodges and Carter, like two dogs after a bitch in heat. He could imagine how they might have perked up at Jenny's appeal, but he thought they were over-doing it. As he had said, they got their pot a-boilin' too easy. They were the troublemaking kind, so it might not take much to set them off in another way as well, with the six-shooters they carried. They were new-grown-up and feeling their oats, trying to prove something. They were big enough to push their way into a man's world, old enough to do damage but not mature enough to have judgment or restraint. He didn't like them; he knew that. He also knew he wasn't going to leave just because they wanted him to. He wasn't going to be pushed away by two young toughs any more than he would be pushed away by some Peeping Tom in a brown suit.

Back at his camp, Felver thought that the thing he should do was pack up his camp and head west. It had been almost a full day since he had stopped at the Blue Horse Saloon. He looked at the sky and saw the sun almost overhead. He looked around at his camp. By the time he got it all packed up and loaded onto the horse, he would have only half a day of travel, and that would be in the warmest part of the day. It seemed like a lot of work for a little gain. Thinking of it in another way, he figured he had three full days of travel before he made it to Fielding's place, so he would have the same number of nights out whether he pulled up right now or stayed till morning. He nodded. He could stay. That would give him a chance to slip into town and see Jenny again.

There was a little bit of lukewarm coffee in the pot, so he drank a cup and chewed the last couple of mouthfuls as he thought of some way to pass the time. He decided to oil his saddle, as it had been rained on a couple of times lately. With the bedding and canvas he made a mound to set the saddle on, and then he scrubbed it dry with an old sock. The leather on the skirts had not yet begun to curl, so that was good. He dug through his gear and found a can of oil he had bought before leaving home. He pried it open with the prong on an extra cinch buckle, and for a moment he admired the clear, dark pool of oil. He was tempted to stick his finger in it, but instead he wiped off a twig and used it to stir the oil. With the old sock, he dipped into the can and daubed oil on the saddle. He liked the rich smell of the oil and then the leather as he crouched in the warming sun and continued his work.

He had just tapped the lid back onto the can when he heard the sound of hooves on dry ground. Looking out toward the area where he had picketed the horses, he saw a lone rider coming his way. The man rode easy in the saddle, and when Felver stood up and walked to the edge of his camp, the rider waved. Felver waved back.

The rider came on in and dismounted a few yards from the spot where Felver stood. He was a cowpuncher from the looks of him, about Felver's own age, and he had an easygoing air about him. He wore a wide-brimmed gray hat with a tall crown, and he had on a loose, billowy shirt. The man seemed to be naturally high-chested, as if he had just taken a deep breath of air. He wore no vest but instead had a pocket and flap sewn onto his shirt on the left side. For the rest of his outfit he wore faded denim pants and black boots with the tops of the toes well worn.

"What say?" said Felver.

"Not much. Saw your horses and your camp, so I thought I'd stop in and say hello." The man spoke with what sounded like a Texas accent.

"Glad you did."

"My name's Dalhart. Jim Dalhart."

"Pleased to meet you. Mine's Owen Felver."

"Mighty fine."

As they shook hands, Felver got an impression of Dalhart's blue eyes, straight brown hair, wide cheekbones, eagle nose, and large teeth. The man was a smiler.

"Well, come in and set awhile," Felver offered.

"Might as well." Dalhart dropped his reins and walked to the campsite with Felver. The horse, apparently well trained to being ground-hitched, did not move.

"Not much shade," Felver said.

"Don't need much." Dalhart smiled, and his left hand went up to his pocket, where he drew out a bag of tobacco and a pack of papers. He made a gesture of offering a smoke to Felver, who declined. Dalhart rolled a cigarette, licked it and tapped it, then lit it and tossed the match in the fire pit.

Felver pointed to a little patch of shade on the south side of the chokecherry bushes. "We could sit over there," he said.

"Good enough."

The two men sat down, Felver with his butt on the ground and his arms hooked around his knees, and Dalhart squatting with his right knee lower than his left and a forearm draped on each knee.

36

"Slippin' into summer, sure enough," Dalhart said as he brought the cigarette up to his mouth. "Country's startin' to turn dry."

Felver thought of his summer job, still three days away. "Yep," he said. He looked at Dalhart, who was gazing off to the southeast, where the dry grass sloped up and away from the creek. He figured the cowpuncher had ridden across some open range and had waited to light a smoke. "You work around here?" he asked.

Dalhart looked back at him and tipped an ash from his cigarette. "Uh-huh. I work for a fella named George Percy, off to the north and west of here."

"How's he?"

"All right. He's fair. He's just gettin' started, so he doesn't have a very big outfit."

"Not one of the big shots, then."

Dalhart laughed. "No, he sure isn't." He looked around at his horse and then back. "I don't know if he even wants to be."

"Takes a certain type, doesn't it?"

"I 'magine." Dalhart took a drag on his cigarette and blew out the smoke. "How 'bout yourself? Are you just passin' through?"

Felver shrugged. "I guess so. I camped here last night, and I'll probably stay at least one night more."

Dalhart yawned and nodded. "Nice enough place."

Felver remembered Jenny saying close to the

same thing, and he had an image of her as he had seen her last, walking into the hotel. "Uh-huh."

Dalhart wrinkled his nose and took another drag. "Water and all."

When Dalhart finished his cigarette, he said he needed to be moving along. He stood up, ground out his cigarette stub with his heel, shook hands with Felver, and walked back to his horse, which had not moved from its spot. He gathered the reins, swung into the saddle in his easy way, waved, and said, "So long."

As Dalhart rode away, Felver went out to take a look at his horses. Finding everything in order, he went back to sit in the shade. He thought about his recent visitor. Dalhart seemed friendly enough, and he didn't seem to be up to anything more than just dropping in to say hello. Anyone who had cattle out on the open range might want to take a look at strangers passing through. Dalhart hadn't asked any prying questions, and he had probably found out as much as he felt he needed to know.

Felver scratched at the ground with a stick. There wasn't much to do at a time like this. He knew some fellows who were forever cleaning a gun, sharpening a knife, or fixing things that didn't need to be fixed, but he didn't have a compulsion to be tinkering. Still, after a certain amount of sitting around, he could get bored, especially when he knew there was a girl in town he'd like to see again.

Before long he had the newly oiled saddle cinched down on the chestnut horse, and leaving the brown packhorse by itself once again, he headed for town. The ride took only about twenty minutes, so the sun was still overhead as he rode down the main street. He noted the relative locations of the hotel, the café, the Blue Horse Saloon, the barbershop, the butcher shop, the mercantile, the livery stable, and Five Star Drayage. Coper's business was in the middle of a block on the north of the street, two blocks west of the café and saloon. He imagined Coper went home for midday dinner, and again he wondered which house he lived in.

Felver decided he would go to the mercantile store. He had stocked up on all the normal supplies before he left the Wolf River country, so he didn't need any personal items for himself. But he thought he might like to buy a scarf or handkerchief for Jenny, just something to remember him by, before he left town.

, The clerk was a young man with a high collar and a neatly trimmed mustache. Felver imagined Heid would look that way if he sent his suit to the cleaners and went to the barbershop. The clerk was a model of discretion when he learned that Felver was looking for "something for a lady." The clerk spoke in a low voice and gave knowing nods. After a few minutes, Felver heard the doorbell tinkle. The clerk excused himself and said he would be back in a few minutes.

Felver was looking at the handkerchiefs laid out on the counter when he heard the clerk's voice.

"Good afternoon, Mrs. Coper. What can I help you with?"

A little jolt ran through Felver's shoulders and neck. He turned to his left and saw a sight that took him by surprise.

It was an obese woman with puffy arms and a pasty, swollen face. She had dark, inset eyes, and her light brown hair was cut off even, all the way around, halfway to her shoulders. Felver could see her white neck, and he thought she must spend very little time outside. From her shoulders down, her dress was like a tent with a center pole; it spread out on all sides and then hung down. The fabric was dark blue, with some kind of a print in it that was hard to see in the dim light.

Felver heard her voice but could not make out the words. Then he heard the clerk's louder voice.

"Not until next week, I'm afraid. But we expect a full shipment and a good selection."

Mrs. Coper said something, and the clerk laughed.

"Yes, it should come in on one of his wagons, all right. I would expect it on Monday."

Felver looked at the woman. He thought she was probably of average height but looked shorter because of her body. He felt sorry for

40

her, but he also felt relieved that he hadn't had any closer dealings with her. Even at this distance, the sight of her made him feel discomfort.

Mrs. Coper said something and turned to leave. The clerk thanked her for stopping in, and then he came back to Felver and the handkerchiefs.

"I think I'll take this one here."

"The lavender one? Yes, that's very nice. Very pretty." The young man in the high collar looked at Felver. "Would you like me to wrap it?"

"Sure. That would be fine."

The clerk began to wrap the folded handkerchief in plain paper. Felver watched as he folded and tucked the paper, then pulled off a length of string and tied the little bundle both ways. It looked rather flimsy, but the handkerchief was folded up as much as it should be, and Felver wasn't going to take it very far.

In a few minutes, Felver was back out in the street in the bright daylight. He looked around for Mrs. Coper but did not see her. His brief view of her had been strange and unreal, he thought. He had seen her well enough to know her again by sight, but he would have liked to see her in better light, to try to make more sense out of her appearance. He had a vague notion that there was something he didn't understand about this town of Cameron, and he felt it was worth understanding even if he

41

wasn't going to be around for long.

He stepped out into the open street and headed for the café. Having seen Mrs. Coper in the store, and remembering what Jenny had told him, he now felt that the eye of the town was on him. The eye of the clerk probably was, at least, as he had made a conspicuous purchase and was on his way to the café where the new girl worked.

Once inside the café, he saw that only one table on the right was occupied. It looked as if the dinner hour had ended, as some tables still had dirty dishes on them. The man at the cash box didn't seem inclined to get up and clear any of them. He sat with a wide-eyed stare and smoked his cigar.

Felver took a clean table on the left side and sat down. Pretty soon Jenny came to his table. She was still wearing the gray dress, but she didn't look bad. She smiled and said hello, and he did the same.

"Dinner or just coffee?"

"Well, I'm not all that hungry. I haven't done much today. I think I could get by on a cup of coffee and a slab of pie, if you have it."

"I'm sorry," she said. "All the pie is gone."

"Well, I'll just have coffee, then."

When she came back with the coffee, he set the little package on the corner nearest her. She looked down at it.

"It's for you," he said. "Don't worry. It's not much. It's just a little thing. I don't know when

I might be leaving, and I wanted you to have something to help you remember me."

She put her hand next to the package and gave him a look that showed worry. "You're not leaving already, are you?"

He shrugged. "Oh, I don't know. I don't really have to, but —"

"No," she said. "Go ahead. You don't have any reason to stay around. I'll get along all right." She looked at him, and he saw a sad, defeated look on her face. "You don't even know me," she said.

"Well, I'd like to," he answered. "But I've just sort of got this other job waiting for me."

"Go ahead. You've been nice to me, and I'll remember that."

He looked at her light blue eyes, and he knew she didn't want him to go. He also knew that he didn't want to go, either. "Nah," he said, shaking his head. "I'm not leaving that soon. I'll stick around at least a couple more days."

She looked happier even as she said, "I don't want you to lose a job over me."

His heart was light and he was happy, now that he had said out loud that he was going to stay. "Don't worry about that. I've never had any trouble finding a job." He glanced at her gift. "But I'd want you to have this, whether I go or stay."

"Thank you," she said, picking up the little package.

"You're welcome. I hope you like it."

"I'm sure I will."

She took the package to the kitchen, and then she went about her work at clearing tables. The man at the cash box smoked his cigar and didn't seem to lose track of her. Felver thought the man might just want to make sure she tended to business, but he couldn't tell. Just about any man would want to look at her at least once.

On his way out of the café, he saw Hodges and Carter riding up the street. He knew they'd like to see him gone, but he wasn't going to give them that satisfaction. He turned right on the sidewalk and walked two blocks until he came to the hotel.

At the desk, he asked the clerk for paper and a pen and ink.

"I'd like to send a letter to Chugwater," he said.

He explained in his letter that it looked as if he was going to have to lay over in Cameron for a little while. He wrote that if Fielding had to hire someone else, or had even done so already, he understood and hoped he had caused no inconvenience. He wished him good luck in his business.

As Felver walked back out onto the sidewalk, he felt as if a weight had lifted. He had looked forward to working with a pack string, but maybe he could do that some other time. For right now, he could just hang around and see what happened.

44

Chapter Three

When the afternoon shadows started to lengthen, Felver thought he might go out and look for some camp meat. He had seen deer sign when he had gone for firewood the day before, and he knew it was antelope country out on the grassland. He liked both kinds of meat, but he favored deer, and in the warm weather it would last a few days longer. With that in mind, he would look for deer first.

He took his rifle out of the tent, checked it for cartridges, and headed off on a slow walk upstream. Once he had camp behind him, the world started to fill in. He could hear the trickle of the creek and the occasional flutter of a bird. Most of the time he walked in the quiet shadows of cottonwoods and box elders. Sometimes chokecherries or other bushes grew down to the water's edge, so he had to go up and around, into the full sunlight of late afternoon, and then back along the creek in mottled shadows.

After a spell of walking he sat for a while, not because he was tired but because he knew he should not move along at one steady pace. He listened to the gurgle of the water and to the clatter of a faint breeze in the cottonwood trees overhead. The world was a fairly simple place at moments like this, when the weather was good and town was far enough away. A fellow didn't need much, most of the time — just some decent grub and clean water, a tent in case of a thunderstorm, and a fire, of course. Well, sometimes it was nice to have a drink, or get close to a woman, now that he thought of it, but those weren't things he needed every day.

He yawned. It seemed he got sleepiest when he wasn't doing anything. He shook his head. He needed to keep himself alert, not only for the hunting but for anything else that might come along. He lifted the rifle from his lap and set it on the ground, with the muzzle resting on a piece of deadfall so that the rifle wouldn't lie in the dirt. Then he pushed himself to his feet and walked to the creek, where he crouched at the water's edge and splashed his face. The water was cool like before, and it left his face feeling clean and fresh.

Always at times like this he expected a bear to rise up or a shot to ring out, but nothing happened except the silent drop of an amber-colored dragonfly, which hovered in front of him for a second and then zapped away.

Back on the hunt, he imagined he had gone about a mile from camp, and he had not seen much beyond the trees and bushes that grew along the creek. He had heard a story about people who had camped on a cold bitter night and had nearly frozen, and then in the morning had found a cozy ranch house just over the next rise. He had also heard a story about a fellow who had had a similar surprise just after he had branded a slick calf. Remembering those stories, Felver could imagine touching off a shot and then finding out he was in somebody's backyard. He figured it was worth the effort to take a look at the surrounding country.

He walked out from the creek, heading north. He followed the ground as it sloped up and away, and after a quarter of a mile he came to the crest of a little rise. He took off his hat and cleared the rim slowly, scanning the country as it came into view.

Nothing remarkable presented itself. The rolling plains stretched away in every direction, with hazy buttes to the northwest and mountains far to the southwest. They would be the Laramie Mountains, he thought, where Fielding would be waiting to hear from him. In the middle distance, all he could see was grassland, with an occasional earth-colored gash or bluff. He did not see a single building or windmill, although he saw dark spots that he was sure were cattle.

Felver walked back to the creek and followed it west again. The sun was in his eyes part of the time now, so he pulled down his hat brim and tried to make use of the taller trees. He was moving through a grove of half-grown cottonwoods when he saw movement ahead and to his left. He stopped. It was a deer, crossing the creek and moving into the trees ahead of him. Now the deer had stopped, for there was no movement. Felver held his rifle upright in front of him, so as not to have any unnatural shapes sticking out. Keeping a tree between himself and where he thought the deer was, he took soft steps forward. When he came to the tree he brought the rifle down and rested its barrel with his left hand on the tree trunk. The deer stepped into view, one slow step at a time. It was about sixty yards away.

Felver saw a sprig of forked-horn antlers, still in velvet, barely sticking above the large mule ears. It was a young buck, sleek and healthy. Felver looked it over, front quarters and back. There were some good steaks there, and not so much would go to waste as on a big deer. Lining up the sights on the deer's brisket behind its front leg, he squeezed the trigger.

The shot crashed in the still afternoon, and the deer gave one leap before it crumpled. Felver backed away from the tree and walked toward the deer. It gave a few kicks, but by the time he reached it, there was no fight left. He had made a good, clean kill.

With his pocketknife he made a quick job of opening up the abdomen and tumbling out the guts. As he did so he appreciated the young, white fat that lay along the kidneys. This deer was in good shape, and getting him cleaned right away would help keep the meat from spoiling. The heart and lungs pulled out without much resistance on a young one like this, and Felver made a clean trim on the other end as well. When he was done with the field dressing, he dragged the carcass away from the gut pile. He thought the fresh, glistening heap might attract scavengers before he got back with a horse, and he would rather that a magpie or coyote stick to the fresh innards. As he washed his hands and forearms in the creek, he felt satisfied with the neat job he had been able to make of the task.

The packhorse seemed glad to be taken off his picket. Felver gave him a quick rubdown and then slipped on the pad, packsaddle, and breeching. Next he made short work of saddling the other horse, and the sun was still hanging in the western sky when he brought the horses to the site of the kill.

After a couple of sashays and spills, Felver wrestled the deer onto the packhorse and tied it on. Then he mounted the saddle horse, gave a tug on the lead rope, and got the horses moving back toward camp. He took a look back at the gut pile, which had not been bothered yet, and he had the pleasant thought that he might make some coyote happy.

Back at camp, he decided to hang the deer in the cottonwoods overnight and then to stash it in the shade during the day. He was hungry, and he didn't want to skin the deer in the dark, so he cut out the tenderloins from inside the ribs and beneath the soft white fat, and he built a fire. With a scrap of bacon he greased the skillet, and then he fried up a panful of juicy little steaks. Enjoying his meal by firelight, he could think of only a couple of things that would have made the evening better.

In the morning, after skinning the deer and finding the meat cool to the touch, he cut out a strip of the backstrap and set it aside, then wrapped the carcass in a canvas sheet and laid it on the dirt floor of his tent. He covered the bundle with his canvas packs, and his ground sheet after that, to keep in the coolness.

He was hungry, and as he went about his work he remembered something he had seen once in Omaha, in a restaurant. The man at the table next to him had a plate containing nothing but a large boneless steak, seared and steaming, and a dozen shiny sections of cut oranges. There must have been two or three oranges, and the steak must have weighed a pound.

Felver smiled. It had been a long time since he had eaten an orange, and he didn't know when he might get a chance again, but it was a nice thought. A juicy orange or a cup of fresh strawberries — that would be just it. But he had good eats as it was, and plenty of it. He thought about brother coyote up the creek a mile, nosing out the bloody liver, and he thought everything was fine here on Red Creek.

This time he cut off a larger flitch of bacon and set it skittering in the pan. He cut the chunk of backstrap into four steaks, each one nearly an inch thick and as big around as his fist. He laid them in the hot grease, and as the smell of frying meat mixed with the smell of coffee, he didn't think about oranges any more.

After breakfast he whittled a toothpick and drank more coffee. The sun was up above the cottonwoods again, but he didn't need to do anything or be anywhere. At some point in the day he would like to drop in on Jenny, and he hadn't decided what would be the best time. He didn't like to go into a saloon this early in the day, having learned more than once what it was like to stagger out into a hot, glaring afternoon. He wasn't much for fishing, and he had just washed his feet a couple of days earlier. As he ran his hand across his face, it occurred to him that he could shave.

He had a small mirror not much bigger than a silver dollar, but he had learned to use it for his purposes. As he spruced himself up, he recalled Coper's remark about stacking wheat. It must have been the light-colored hair and mustache. Coper must have looked at him and thought he saw a Swede or German or something. Felver smiled. He couldn't worry too much about what Coper thought about him on the basis of his appearance. But Jenny, now — that was different. If she didn't like his looks, that would mean something. But as far as he

51

could tell, they seemed to match up all right. They both had an average build, with light-colored features. Whatever there was in a person that registered and responded to others seemed to be working all right in both directions. She might be the daughter of some punkin roller for all he knew, but even if she was, he couldn't see where it mattered much. He remembered his father saying, about some of the dirt-poor nesters who had lean cattle and skinny chickens, that a poor man had a poor way of doing things. There seemed to be some truth to the idea that some people were poor by nature. Not all working-class people were at the same level. But on the other hand, even if she came from that sort of upbringing, she did work for a living, just like he did, so at the worst she wasn't any lower than the fat-hungry nesters. And it did go lower, he knew that.

Well, he thought as he folded his razor, a fellow had to find out. He didn't think she came from the kind of folks that messed in the yard and didn't bury it, like the McCabes back home. They had low class in their blood, and they were all thin and dirty-haired and didn't seem to care. That was the thing about this girl. She had a good physical presence, and she had her own self-respect.

Once he had gotten shaved, he thought it wouldn't hurt him to clean up a little more, so he took off his shirt, sloshed it in the creek, squeezed it out as dry as he could, and spread it on a buffalo berry bush to dry. Then he knelt at the water's edge and washed his face, ears, neck, and arms. His bare skin looked strange to him, gleaming white in the open sunlight. He felt about as clean as he was going to get without taking a dunk in a bathtub at the barbershop.

By the time his shirt was dry, the sun had crossed over into early afternoon. He took his time saddling the horse, and then he let the horse walk at its own pace into town. It was a warm, still afternoon, and the world seemed like a place where not much was likely to happen.

Once inside the café, he stood by the door for a few minutes. He did not see Jenny, and he was worried at seeing another woman serving the meals. She was a drab, blocky woman with brown hair pulled back into a single braid. Her face glistened with perspiration, and she was breathing hard when she came up to ask Felver how she could help him.

He found the nerve to ask if Jenny was around. The woman said she was but she was in the kitchen washing dishes. Felver glanced at the man at the cash box and wondered if there was any motive behind the change. He figured there was nothing he could do about it anyway, so he said he would come back later.

Remembering the cold beer he had had two days earlier, he went to the Blue Horse Saloon. Once inside, he looked at a dark corner to adjust his eyes. Then he walked to the bar and asked for a beer. Turning from the bar to look over the room, he saw Heid and another man sitting at a table in dim light, up against the wall. Heid waved and motioned him over, so he carried his beer to the table. Both of the other men had half-full whiskey glasses, and a bottle sat between them.

Heid introduced the other man as Dave McNair. Felver shook his hand and sat down. Despite a short-billed cap that might have come off the streets of Chicago, McNair was a primitive-looking sort. He had thick, sandy-colored hair and a full face of dirty stubble that made his eyes look sunken. He had gaps between his yellow teeth, and his jaw hung agape. He was not old — maybe a year or two older than Heid — but his head seemed heavy as it leaned forward.

"What kind of work do you do?" McNair lifted a soggy-ended cigarette to his mouth as he stared at Felver.

"Oh, sort of an all-around hand. Ranch work and such. Thinkin' about bein' a packer." Felver looked at his two new companions. "How 'bout you fellas?"

McNair looked at Heid, and the cigarette danced in his mouth as he said, "See? You oughta talk to him."

Felver turned a dubious look at Heid. "You don't pack, do you?"

Heid let the ends of his mustache go down

as he said, "Oh, no."

Felver said, "Oh," with a bit of trailing off, to invite explanation.

Heid put on a serious look and said, "I've studied photography."

"Oh," said Felver. "Have you got a shop here in town?"

"No, I haven't. But I'd like to set one up."

"Uh-huh." Felver sipped on his beer. He didn't know how much of Heid to believe. The man seemed like a loafer as much as anything.

"Heid's real smart," McNair piped up.

Felver looked at Heid.

Heid looked at McNair and smirked. "So I've studied a little. I know more about exposures than anyone in this town." Then, as if he had wasted a joke on McNair, he looked at Felver and said, "I've had training in all of it — like exposing the plates and developing the pictures. I can do all the work in the darkroom, but I think my real talent is in taking the pictures. I've got a good sense of perspective."

McNair spoke up again. "My idea of a good darkroom is a vault."

Heid gave a quizzical look. "You mean like an underground chamber?"

McNair looked at him as if he were a moron. "Hell, no, I don't mean a burial vault. I mean a bank vault." The cigarette danced in his mouth as he laughed at his own joke.

"Well, some darkrooms are down underground, so it was a reasonable question for me to ask." Heid put on a bored look and picked up his pipe where it lay on the table. He put the stem in his mouth, lit a match, and produced a cloud of smoke. The flame lit up his features for a moment, and then he sank back into the shadowy light. He looked at Felver and said, "You see, I've got the equipment and I know how to use it, but I need to find a way to get it here."

Felver took another sip. "Where is it?"

Heid took the pipe out of his mouth. "St. Louis."

Felver raised his eyebrows. "That's a ways." Then a thought crossed his mind as he remembered the first time he had seen Heid. "Isn't Coper in that line of business?"

McNair gave a short, snide laugh.

"What's the matter?" Felver asked.

McNair took the cigarette out of his mouth, and with his chin jutting up and down he said, "Anyone with a lick of sense wouldn't let him haul anything more fragile than a dead cow." McNair jerked his head in the direction of the bar. "He's proud as hell that he shipped in the bar and mirror and cabinets, but it's not his fault it all got here in one piece."

Felver looked at the bar and mirror, then back at Heid. He remembered that Heid had not professed great friendship with Coper, but he also noted that Heid did not say anything directly against him. Felver shrugged. "Well, I don't know. Maybe your equipment is more delicate. I know a fella that says he could pack a whole china shop and not break a teacup."

"Oh?" said Heid, palming the bowl of his pipe. "Where's he?"

"In Chugwater."

"Hell, that's too far away. That can't do me any good."

McNair's voice came up sharp again. "How 'bout you?"

"I'm not really in the business."

Heid blew out more smoke. "I'll find someone. I'm not in that big of a hurry."

McNair snickered. "You're never in a hurry to work."

Heid looked as if he was going to match McNair's sarcasm and then changed his mind. "No need to be," he said.

Felver sat through another beer and listened to the two men banter with one another. At one point McNair rose to a level of seriousness, almost zeal. The sunken eyes fired up as he railed at the rich bastards and how they made their money off the poor workingman. He was damned if he was going to help them get richer. Heid said he thought they might make it without McNair's help. McNair's fire went down and he acted sullen for a few minutes, until the banter picked up again.

From all of the small talk, Felver did not get the idea that McNair had any line of work except living off his wits. He seemed to consider himself pretty well furnished in that area, and

Heid's barbed comments did not seem likely to change McNair's impression of himself. Felver realized that much of the exchange was for his benefit, and it wasn't any worse than listening to two Texans arguing about the best way to fight a Mexican.

After finishing his second beer, Felver got up and took leave.

"Come back in again," said Heid. "You're staying around here, aren't you?"

Felver looked at them both. He had the impression that they both knew the answer already. "Yes, I am," he said. "I'm camped on the creek, about a mile out of town."

McNair gave a little heh-heh. "Well, we know where to find you, then, if we need someone to pack in something."

Felver was about to answer when he realized McNair was setting up a joke, so he just nodded.

McNair went ahead. "We're thinkin' of puttin' in a whorehouse, and we'll need some knockers. Heid and I'll take care of the knickers."

Felver smiled. "I don't think you'll have to go all the way to St. Louis. I believe you can find some of those things in Cheyenne."

Back in the café, Felver saw that the dinner crowd had been there and gone, and the bald man with the cigar was nowhere in sight. Jenny sat alone at a table near the kitchen, eating a bowl of stew. As Felver walked up to her table, she invited him to sit down.

She was wearing a white apron over a pale blue dress, and her hair was tied in back. A few loose hairs hung out, and her face was shiny with light perspiration.

"Did they change your job?" he asked.

"Yes, and it's just as well. Those two good-for-nothings would come in and sit for hours, with no end to their comments, so Mr. Garth put me in the kitchen. I help the cook and wash dishes." She brushed a loose hair away from her eyebrow. "But I don't mind it." She looked around and then said in a lower voice, "This isn't goin' to last forever anyway."

"I guess not."

"How about yourself?" She ate a spoonful of stew.

"Just the same. Not goin' anywhere right away."

She nodded and swallowed. "Still in the same place?"

"Oh, yeah." He saw her eyes rove a little, and he was glad he had taken the trouble to clean up.

"Well," she said, "I'm glad you dropped in. This joint gets kind of dreary, especially in the kitchen." Then she added, "But like I said, I don't mind it if I know it's goin' to get me somewhere."

Felver wanted to ask where she thought she might go next, but he couldn't think of the right way to say it without being personal.

"Well, it's work," he said.

"That's right. And like they say, the money's good. Just not enough of it."

Felver laughed. He liked the girl's cheerfulness, and he didn't mind her casual manner and not standing on ceremony with her language. She carried it well. "What time of day do you get out of here?" he asked.

"Usually about nine. So far, I've been so dog-tired that I just go back to my room and expire."

"Well, if I'm going to be hanging around a few days more, and you're going to be doing the same, we ought to see about having a cup of coffee or something."

Her face brightened. "The morning's a better time for me, as things go right now."

Felver nodded. "As for a place, I don't suppose you'd want to come right back in here on your time off."

"It wouldn't be the most enjoyable."

"Well, you could take your chance at havin' breakfast at my place again."

She smiled. "I didn't get sick last time."

They made a date for the following morning, and Felver got up to leave her to her meal and her work.

Felver rode out of town in the middle of the afternoon. Not much seemed to be going on at that time of day. A few horses stood drowsing at the hitching rails, but not a wagon could be seen in the main street. The weather was warm enough, and he imagined most people were holed up inside. Heid and McNair were probably still at their dusky table in the Blue Horse Saloon. He imagined Coper at his desk, behind the false front and wooden overhang of Five Star Drayage, and he pictured Mrs. Coper inside a dark house, maybe padding slowly from one room to the other.

Felver looked up at the sky. There was not a cloud in sight, just the bright sun shining down. He remembered days like this in the past — hot summer days when he was on day herd, drowsing in a world of flies and dust and the smell of a thousand cattle. He didn't mind a little time off right now, even if he was losing wages. He knew he would be back at it soon enough.

Halfway out to his camp, he saw two riders come over a rise from the northwest. He recognized them as Hodges and Carter. He wondered if they had been waiting for him, or if they had been off to no good out on the range. He saw that Carter was wearing a red shirt, which meant that the pair wasn't trying very hard to stay out of sight. As the two rode closer, Felver looked to see if they carried ropes. He didn't see any on the left side, and then as the horses made a turn to go around a prairie dog mound, he saw that the men had no ropes on the right side, either. That meant they weren't giving the impression of being range riders.

"Good afternoon," he said as the two riders came to a stop. He saw they were both wearing side arms as before.

"Same to you," said Carter. Then, after a moment of silence, he said, "I see you're still around."

"Not a hard thing to see," Felver answered.

"Well, aren't we smart?" came in Hodges's voice.

"Maybe," said Felver.

Carter spoke again, his face like a hard knot. "We thought a smart man would be gone by now."

"Must be just your way of thinkin', then."

Carter gave him another hard look. "You do think you're pretty smart. I wonder how good you are with your fists."

Felver could feel himself getting mad. Carter knew how to make a man want to fight. It was the narrow, tight look he gave and the taunting tone in his voice. Felver took a breath and let it out. "Good enough, I'd guess."

Hodges came off his horse in a smooth motion and stood out in front with the reins in his right hand. "Well, come on, then."

That was the way it was, then. Carter got things started, and then they switched it over to Hodges. Felver looked at the droopy eyes, fat lips, and sagging gut, and he thought the fellow must be better than he looked if that was the way the two of them worked things.

"Don't put yourself out," Felver said, looking

Hodges in the eye. "Your partner here is the one that called me out. I'm not goin' to fight you both, unless he turns out to be real easy." Felver looked at Carter, with his knee-high boots and wrist cuffs and clean shirt. His shaded face looked like a light-colored plum, but he didn't look like he wanted to fight.

"You're pretty cocky," said Carter. "You're not likely to make many friends around here."

"I don't need many, least like you."

"We'll see," said Carter with a tight nod. He gathered his reins and turned his horse to the left.

Hodges made a smooth mount and turned out with his fellow rider. His hand brushed his six-gun as if by habit to check that it was still there, and then he touched spurs to his horse and was gone with his partner.

Chapter Four

The man from Wolf River poked at the venison steaks as they sputtered in the greased skillet. They were brown on one side and cooking well on the other. As soon as the blood came to the top he would flip the steaks again and start making the gravy. He looked at the Dutch oven nestled in the coals, and he could imagine the biscuits expanding inside. They would go well with the meat and gravy. The smell of coffee wafted in the air and mixed with the smell of bacon grease and fried meat. The last of his bacon had gone to a good cause.

He looked across the campfire and smiled at Jenny, who sat on her canvas cushion and held a tin cup of coffee on her lap. Her hair was clean, and her light blue eyes were clear and shining. Her pink blouse was wrinkled, as if it had come out of a valise, but it fit her just right and made Felver appreciate her features. She wore brown corduroy trousers, which he imagined she chose so that she could sit comfortably in camp and ride a horse back to town. Best of all, he thought, was the lavender-colored handkerchief she had tied loosely around her neck.

Felver looked at the sun above the cotton-woods and enjoyed the leisure of the moment. Sometimes he missed work and the company of friends, but he did not miss the hurry of some jobs, such as roundup, when a man had to bolt his food and rush back to work. He ate fast when he had to, but when it came to the old question of whether life was a matter of work to eat or eat to work, he thought that working to eat was the only sensible way to look at it.

He poked at the steaks again with the tip of his jackknife blade, and the sizzling increased. The juice was coming to the top now. He stabbed and turned the steaks one by one, then poured in the flour and water for the gravy.

"What do you think?" he asked, looking her way again.

"Looks pretty good. You seem to know what you're doing."

"I try." With his knife he scooted the steaks around in the gravy, which was still white and thin. Without looking at her he said, "You ever cook much?"

"No, not much. But I can get by. I can boil spuds without burnin' 'em."

He looked at her and saw her smiling. He smiled back. "That's nice." He looked back at the skillet, and as he poked some more he said, "What else do you think?"

"It takes a big coon to drown a dog."

He looked up. "Is that right?"

"I guess so. I don't really know. It's just something my brother would say when someone asked him what he thought."

"Oh. Is he a coon hunter?"

"Oh, yeah. Sometimes I think he lives for it."

Felver thought she might not object to a halfway personal question at this point, so he asked, "Where does he hunt coons?"

"Right there out of Terre Haute."

"Is that where you're from?" He looked at her, but he didn't see anything distinctive that suggested Indiana.

She nodded.

"You came a little ways, then. It's different here."

She shrugged. "In some ways. The air's not so heavy here, and a body can sleep at night."

"Uh-huh. I suppose things are a lot more modern there, too."

"Oh, some things, like telephones and electric lights, but Cheyenne's got just about everything Terre Haute does."

"You get very far from Cheyenne, though, and a lot of that ends pretty quick."

"Yes, but if you didn't have it to begin with, you don't miss it. You eat the same. You sleep the same. I even wash dishes the same as I did there."

Felver looked at her again. "Doesn't sound like you miss it very much."

She turned down her mouth and shook her head. "No, I don't. It seemed like all I ever saw growin' up was drinkin' and fightin'."

Felver gave a nervous laugh. "Well, I guess it's not all that different here." After a thought he said, "I suppose it's how you live."

"I guess so. I thought all I wanted out of life was to be somewhere where people weren't getting drunk and bickering with each other all the time." She took a sip of her coffee and went on. "I thought I met someone who wanted the same thing, but actually, he wanted something else."

Felver didn't have much to say. He almost felt criticized until he realized she meant that that was all the other fellow had wanted. "That's too bad," he said. "There's some nice things to get out of life, and they don't cost all that much."

He looked at her, and her face was still soft. She didn't seem to be hardened by the life she had seen, and she didn't seem to be reworking any bitterness.

"I believe it," she said. "It just seems so hard, and so many people willing to get in the way."

"You mean people like them young trouble-makers? I bumped into them again, by the way. Nothin' to speak of, though."

"Well, yes, them. But I was also thinking of people like Mr. Coper, or even Mr. Garth. They don't seem to think a girl should enjoy anything."

"I wouldn't have thought to connect them, but they both do seem to have a jealous eye."

She let out a sigh. "All I know is, I won't mind leaving when the time comes."

Felver took a chance with his next question. "How long will that be?"

"You tell me," she said. "Almost half of what

I make goes for room rent, and I don't even have my next place figured out."

Felver raised his eyebrows. "I couldn't tell you right now," he said, "but don't do anything sudden without lettin' me know." He looked at her and gave her a wink. "I'd want to help you get past the wolf pack, at least."

She smiled, and her eyes twinkled. "I'm sure I could use your help. So don't you go running off without telling me, either."

"It's a deal," he said. He scooted the steaks again. "This gravy's thickening up just right, and I'd bet those biscuits are just about ready."

Jenny rode the saddle horse back to town, while Felver rode the packhorse bareback. Once in town, he helped her dismount and walked her into the hotel. They touched hands lightly, and then they parted.

Back in the street, he felt again as if the eye of the town was on him. He mounted the saddle horse and pulled on the lead rope of the second horse. He would have ridden in the middle of the street, but he saw a ranch wagon coming in from the west, so he rode in the right half of the street. As he approached the block where Five Star Drayage was located, he saw the door open inward. The wooden overhang cast the door and windows in shade. A person walked out, and it proved to be Coper.

He called out Felver's name.

Trying to shrug off the feeling of dread that

passed through his upper body, Felver turned his horse in the direction of the building. He was sure Coper had watched him ride into town, leave off his companion, and ride back.

Coper stood on the sidewalk, still in the shade, wearing a brown suit and hat like before. His eyes were not visible, but his spade beard was. "I won't detain you more than a minute," he said. "I'm sure you have somewhere to go."

"What is it?" Felver tried to make his tone sound civil.

"I want to warn you about that girl."

"What about her?"

"She's a dangerous one. She can get you in trouble."

"Is that right?" Felver could see the man's eyes now. They were almost on a level with his, as the sidewalk was up from the street.

"Yes, I think she has delusions, or something. I heard from Heid that you had dropped in to see her a couple of times, and I just wanted to warn you."

"Well, I guess you've done that." Felver wondered how much Coper had heard and how much he had seen for himself.

"I don't blame you for being a bit cross. I'm sorry for that misunderstanding we had the other day." As Coper spoke, Felver could see his eyes roving to take in the rider and two horses.

"Think nothing of it," Felver said.

"Very well."

Felver was about ready to touch spurs to the horse when Coper spoke again.

"They say you're a packer."

"Not much of one, really."

"Well, sometimes I'm looking for someone in that line. I'll keep you in mind."

"Never hurts."

The eyes were on him now. "Do you have work?"

Felver thought of the dirty dishes back at camp and said, "That's where I'm headed right now."

Coper glanced over the two horses again and said, "Good enough. I won't keep you. It's been a pleasure talking to you."

"Likewise." Felver touched his hat brim and moved the two horses back into the middle of the street.

On his way back to camp, Felver thought about the encounter he had just had. He couldn't believe that Coper was sincere, and he couldn't believe that Coper would even think he had been taken in by the friendly warning and the offer of work. He wondered what the man's real motives were. Maybe Coper did want to reduce the animosity, and maybe he wanted to know if Felver had a job to keep him around. Whatever the motive, Coper still didn't shape up as someone worth trusting.

Felver turned it over a little more. Coper made for an interesting study in comparison with Hodges and Carter. They were more overt in their methods, but Coper would probably like to see him gone just as much as they did. Felver laughed as he thought about the possibility of leaving and taking the girl with him. He wondered what the others would think of that.

Later in the afternoon, after washing the cookware and the eating utensils, Felver spent a pleasant hour making a pot hook. First he had to find a chokecherry branch that had a strong branch forking off of it. After cutting the branch just below the fork, he cut off the smaller branch about two inches from the base. That would be the hook he would use to lift the lid off the pot or to lift the pot out of the coals. Next he cut off the main branch at about thirty inches. After that he took his time at the small work of peeling off the bark and trimming the hook so it would slip in and out of the welded ring handle on the pot lid. Making a pot hook was a pleasant task by itself, and it was all the more enjoyable because it gave him free time to think about Jenny. They had had a nice meal and a talk, and he hadn't gotten any signals that he wasn't comfortable with.

As the afternoon shadows began to reach out from the chokecherry thicket, Felver wondered what he might do to help pass the time. It would be a few hours before he would hang out the deer again, as he had done the night before. His camp was clean, and he had biscuits for the evening. He looked around and decided he could go for more firewood. After taking the horses for a drink and putting them back out to

71

graze, he picked up the ax and went west along the creek.

He found more wood where he had found the first batch, and the exertion of swinging the ax made him feel good. Soon he had enough for a couple of more fires, so he gathered up an armload and carried it to camp. When he got there, he was surprised to find a visitor.

It was Dalhart, crouched in the shade of the tent and smoking a cigarette. He was dressed as before, with the same shirt and sewn-on pocket.

"Good afternoon," said Felver.

"Same to you. I thought you'd be back pretty soon, when I heard the wood-choppin' come to an end."

Felver dropped the firewood by the remnants of his first stack. "I've got to go get the rest, along with the ax. Just wait here and relax."

When Felver came back again, Dalhart had his cigarette snuffed out and his forearms resting on his knees.

Dalhart stood up. "Got it all?"

Felver nodded as he dropped the firewood and ax by the stack. He motioned with his hand that they could sit down. Dalhart went back into his crouch as Felver sat on his butt with his knees raised in front of him.

After a moment, Dalhart spoke. "One day rolls along just about like another, doesn't it?"

"Sure does. Are they keepin' you busy out your way?"

"Some. This fella I work for, he's always got a lot of work laid out."

"Well, that's not the worst kind, I guess."

"No, it's all right. Work don't scare me."

"Me neither, unless it's workin' with dynamite."

Dalhart laughed. "Well, we're not doin' any of that. We're at the stage right now where the boss wants to git things built."

"Like buildings and corrals?"

"That sort of thing. We're just about finished with what he wants to get done at the home place, and he wants to go throw up a couple things at the other place."

"Oh, has he got two places?"

"Sort of. This other fella that works there, name of Prunty, filed on a quarter section just west of here about five miles."

"On the creek?"

"Uh-huh."

Felver nodded. It was a common practice to have a hired hand file on a good claim, especially one that had water, and then turn it over to the boss when it got proved up and the title was clear.

Dalhart took out his bag of makin's and started to build another smoke. "So he wants to do his improvements right now, while he's got a chance. He hasn't got a lot of cattle to look after so far, and he wants to get a shack and a corral throwed up before we go to fall roundup." Dalhart licked the paper and tapped the seam.

"He's actually makin' real improvements, then, not just plowin' a border and callin' it a fence."

Dalhart struck a match and lit his smoke. "Oh, yeah. He aims to use the place."

"Just where is it, then?"

Dalhart looked around and found a twig, then smoothed out the dirt in front of him with his bare hand. "Here's the creek," he said, scratching a long line east and west. "Here's where we are, and here's Prunty's claim, about five miles west of here. And here's Percy's place, north and west of here."

"How far?"

"About seven miles."

Felver studied the scratches in the dirt. "I see. That would give him a line camp, of sorts, even if he doesn't own everything in between."

Dalhart set his hat back on his head. "That's the idea." He took a long drag on his cigarette.

Felver nodded. It made good sense, and it was well within the law. Some of the bigger outfits went at it in a more aggressive way, having their men take up claims in as many good spots as they could, and then pinching out the little outfits when they could.

Dalhart spoke again. "How 'bout you? Are you any good at that sort of thing?"

Felver cocked his head. "What sort?"

"Workin' with lumber. Butcherin' planks and bendin' nails."

"Oh, well, I suppose."

Dalhart held out his cigarette and looked at it, and then he looked at Felver. "The boss wants to hire another hand, to get the job done quicker and not be away from the home place so long."

"Uh-huh."

"It'd be him and Prunty, and you and me. And Clarence the cook. I think he'd have you and me work together."

Felver laughed. "Is that good?"

"It is for me. That way the boss can work with Prunty." Dalhart's teeth showed in a big smile.

Felver laughed again. "What's wrong with Prunty?"

"Oh, nothin'. He just don't say much."

Felver looked again at the map in the dirt. He could use a few days' wages, and it wouldn't take him too far away. "I guess I could give it a try."

Dalhart looked at the sky. "There's plenty of time to ride out and talk to him."

Felver looked up and nodded. "I'd want to get back here in time for bed." He looked at Dalhart's cigarette, which was smoked about halfway down. "Let me saddle my horse, and we'll get goin'."

George Percy's ranch headquarters consisted of one long, cabinlike building that faced south and a stable that sat to the right or east of the ranch house. Behind the stable lay the corrals.

The main building looked as if it was a few years old, but the stable and corrals had the gleam of newness. Dalhart and Felver had followed a trail northward and then gradually to the west. As they approached the stable, Felver could hear a ringing sound of someone beating metal on metal.

The noise became louder as they rode up to the open door. Dalhart dismounted and motioned for Felver to do the same. They tied their horses at the rail and went to the door of the stable. Inside, a lean man was making vicious blows with a sledgehammer. With his left hand he held an iron rod down on an anvil, which was anchored to a stump in the middle of the workshop area.

Dalhart hollered "Bill!" a couple of times. The man set the hammer and bar on the stump and walked over to the doorway. Dalhart made the introduction, confirming Felver's guess that this was Prunty.

Felver's first impression of the man was that he was a humorless sort. He was weasel-faced and gopher-toothed, with a round head that came down to a point at his chin. What beard he had grew sparsely on his chin; at present he had about a week's worth of stubble. He wore a brown hat with a narrow, pinched crown and a flat brim that bent down in front. He had light brown hair and faded blue eyes, and when he raised his head to look straight at the other men, he squinted. His face did not seem to have any specific age to it. He could have been anywhere from twenty-five to forty.

Felver's second impression was that Prunty was tough. He wore a loose work shirt and a buttoned vest that hung loose, but he looked as if his lean body was hard as iron.

The hat brim went down as Prunty took a bag of tobacco out of his vest pocket and began to roll a cigarette. He rolled it thin and tight, not looking at the other two men or saying a word. The hat brim came up, and he had a squinty, worried look on his face as he licked the cigarette and lit it.

Dalhart, meanwhile, had rolled and lit his own, and he did not seem to think it unusual to have Prunty ignore him. Finally he spoke again. "Where's the boss?"

Prunty was taking a tight pull on his cigarette. When he exhaled, he motioned with his head toward the ranch house.

Dalhart took a big drag and blew smoke out of his nostrils. "Well, I brought him another hand." He flicked a glance toward Felver.

Prunty turned his faded blue eyes at Felver and then back at Dalhart. He put his cigarette makin's back in his vest pocket and motioned again toward the ranch house. He said, "Well, that's where he is," and lifted his cigarette back to his mouth. As he did so, he gave Felver the impression that he didn't smoke for enjoyment but rather because he had to.

Dalhart and Felver both thanked him, and as

77

they walked toward the ranch house, the banging sound started up again. Felver imagined Prunty back at the anvil, smashing the hammer on the iron bar and squinting with each jolt.

Dalhart led them in through the first of two doors, which opened into a sort of vestibule with coat hooks and a washstand. Through an open door on the right, Felver could see a bunkhouse. Dalhart went left, into a kitchen and eating area, which had a door on the west end and one leading outside. Felver imagined the door on his left to be the other door he had seen from the outside.

"Clarence must still be takin' his nap," said Dalhart in a low voice. He nodded and walked softly to the door at the west end.

The door opened, and a man with a hat in his hand stepped out of what must have been his own quarters. "Hello, Jim," he said.

"Afternoon. I brought this here fella I mentioned to you."

As Dalhart made the introduction, Felver took an impression of George Percy. He was an average-looking sort, with brown eyes, brown hair, and a full brown beard. He was of medium height, not handsome and not ugly. He looked about thirty years old, and he had a clear-eyed look to him.

"I suppose Jim has told you what I have in mind."

Felver nodded. "He said you needed some help at building."

"That's right. I can pay a dollar and a quarter a day, plus meals, of course."

"That sounds reasonable."

Percy smiled. "Good. I'm glad I don't have to look any further." He glanced at Dalhart and back at Felver. "I'd like to pull out of here in the morning, after breakfast. Jim and Bill and I can ride out ahead, and we should get there sometime a little later in the morning. Clarence can bring the wagon, and I expect it'll take him over half the day to get there."

"Do you want me to just meet you there, then?"

"Sure. And I'm assuming you'll camp right there with us."

Felver gave it a thought. He would have to get into town and let Jenny know what he was up to, but otherwise he could see no problem. "That's fine," he said. "I've got a little bit of a camp myself, and it shouldn't be too much trouble to move it."

"That's good," said Percy, putting the hat on his head. "Bill's knocking up a couple of tools for us in the shop, and Jim and I have time to put a few things together this evening. You're welcome to stay and eat, of course."

"Thanks, but I'd like to get back to my camp before dark."

"Oh, all right. Then we'll see you sometime tomorrow morning. You know where the place is?"

Felver recalled the layout on Dalhart's map.

"About six miles from town, on the north side of the creek, isn't it?"

Percy smiled. "That's right. You should see two big stacks of lumber there." He held out his hand. "Owen, isn't it?"

Felver shook hands as he answered. "That's right. Owen Felver."

"Well, as Jim says, mighty fine. We'll see you there."

On his way back, Felver decided to go to town first. By the time he rode into the main street, the sun had set. Dusk was closing in. The café was closed, but a light in the back showed that the kitchen work wasn't done yet. He sat on the bench and waited as the evening got darker. After about fifteen minutes, he heard the latch in the door, and Jenny stepped out onto the sidewalk. The latch clicked again as she closed the door behind her.

"Good evening," he said.

She took a quick step back and then said, "Oh, it's you, Owen. You scared me."

"Sorry."

"Oh, it's all right now. You just scared me for a moment."

"Can I walk you some place?"

"Yes, if you'd like. I'm on my way back to my room." As they walked down the sidewalk, she asked, "What brings you to town?"

"I needed to see you."

"Oh?" They passed a lit window, and he

could see her looking his way. Her eyes showed worry.

"Uh-huh. I wanted to tell you I was going to be working a few miles farther out for a little while."

"How long do you think that will be?"

"My guess is a week or two. I'm goin' to hammer a few nails for a fellow named George Percy."

"I don't know him."

"He seems like a good-enough sort."

They passed another lit window, and he appreciated a glimpse of her as she turned again. She looked plain and pretty, as always.

"Well, that sounds good," she said.

"I think so. I won't be too far out, and I thought I should let you know where I'd be."

"I'm glad you did."

They crossed a side street and walked along the next block, veering around a pool of light in front of a saloon he was not familiar with. They walked the rest of the block without speaking, and then they crossed the second side street. Up on the next sidewalk, they stopped before they got to the windows and open door of the hotel. There was enough indirect light for him to put his hands with hers and to see her face.

"Well, I hope to see you again before long," he said.

"I hope so, too." She had a faint smile on her face.

He moved toward her, and her lips met his,

lightly and for only a short moment. He moved back and could see her eyes shining.

"It won't be long at all," he said. "I'll come back into town as soon as I can."

"Good," she said. "I won't go anywhere."

On his way back to his horse, Felver slowed down before he came to the saloon on his left. He thought he might as well take a look inside, so he paused at the doorway and peered in. It was a common-looking saloon. The bar ran from front to back on his right, and a few empty tables sat in the unlit side on his left. It was early yet, and only a half-dozen men stood at the bar. They were all looking down the bar to their left, where someone was speaking in a raised voice. All the men he could see had their backs to him, but he recognized two of them. One of them had knee-high boots and wrist cuffs, and the other was wide and heavy.

Felver shrugged and walked on. At least Hodges and Carter hadn't seen him. Then a thought put a smile on his face. If they didn't hear otherwise, they might think they had succeeded in running him out of town.

He untied his horse and mounted up. As he rode out of town, he thought of Jenny and the moment they had spent outside the hotel. He knew he'd be back as soon as he could, just like he'd told her.

Chapter Five

As Felver packed up his camp the next morning, he was glad to be going to work. The dab of money he would earn would be welcome, and the work itself seemed like an agreeable way to make the money. More than that, he was pleased with the idea of doing something worthwhile. A little bit of loafing was all right, but after a while he had found himself restless and wanting something to do. While it was work season, he thought he should be working.

The deer meat was still in good shape, having hung out for three nights in the cool air and having been stowed away in the warm part of the day. For his various meals he had cut out most of the backstrap, so the front and hind quarters were still undisturbed. He cut them from the carcass, cut out what remained of the backstrap, and discarded the bulky part of the carcass, which consisted of ribs and backbone. Thinking of the packhorse and distance they had to go, he trimmed out the leg, thigh, and shoulder bones from the four quarters. The bundle of meat was considerably smaller now, and lighter — about forty pounds of good, clean, boneless venison.

When he loaded the packhorse, he tied the

canvas bundle of meat, balanced evenly, across the two side packs that held the heavier items of his camp, and then he tied his bedding on top. Taking a last look around his camp and seeing nothing except the discarded tent poles and a small stack of wood by the fire pit, he swung into the saddle and led the packhorse out of camp.

He found the work site without any trouble. The two stacks of lumber were visible from half a mile off, gleaming yellow in the open sunlight. A few minutes later, Felver saw three horses picketed out on the grassland. He imagined Percy and his two hired men had arrived as planned.

As he rode closer, he heard a thudding sound. Closer yet, when the lumber stacks were no longer in the way, he saw Prunty hammering on a wooden stake. It was the fourth stake of what looked like the layout of a cabin or shack. Dalhart was down on all fours, diagonally across from Prunty, no doubt eyeballing the layout to his own satisfaction. Percy stood behind Dalhart, hands at his sides. As Felver rode on in, he felt a little excitement at the beginning of a new job. He watched as Dalhart stood up, took the end of a cloth tape measure from Percy, and walked across to the opposite corner as Prunty straightened up and stood back with his sledge. Dalhart and Percy measured one diagonal, then switched corners and measured the other.

As Felver dismounted, Percy and Dalhart walked over to say good morning. Prunty stayed back, rolling a cigarette.

"You can go ahead and get unloaded," said Percy. "If you want to, you can put your horses out, or Bill can do it."

"I'll do it," Felver answered. He looked at the sky. "What time do you expect your other man to come in with the wagon?"

"Not till midafternoon. But we'll eat good when he gets here."

"That reminds me," said Felver. "I brought along some deer meat that's still in good shape."

Percy looked at Dalhart and smiled. Then he looked back at Felver and smiled again. "Well, you're a good man. Jim was all worried that we'd miss dinner. Wondered why we were carryin' tools and didn't have any room for food." He motioned backward with his head. "Now, Bill, he doesn't care if he misses a meal, but Jim does. And he remembers."

Felver looked at Dalhart, who was showing his good teeth with a smile. "I'm sort of like-minded," he said.

Felver unpacked the horses as the other men went back to work. When he joined them, they had run string around the four stakes. Percy and Dalhart were laying beams on the ground outside the string, and Prunty was hacking with a small mattock to scrape out a footing. The beams were heavy and rough like railroad ties, and Felver imagined they would serve as the foundation.

Within a few minutes, Felver and Dalhart were setting the beams in the footings while Prunty dug another footing down the middle. Percy ran string across the middle to give Prunty a line for measuring the depth of the footing. When they had the beams laid out, Felver and Dalhart carried planks for the flooring. They would carry half a dozen, then mark and cut them square before going for more. Percy held the planks in place while Prunty did the hammering. Some of the planks were bowing already, so Percy sometimes had to strain to hold them in position while Prunty drove heavy blows with the hammer.

The work moved along at a reasonable pace. After a couple of hours, the men took a rest. There was no shade, so they sat on the edge of the new floor. Three of them sat, while Prunty stood a few yards away, rolling and then smoking one of his tight little cigarettes.

"We'll be done in no time," said Dalhart, lighting his own cigarette and then blowing away a cloud of smoke. "You see? We could've gone up to Moran's and helped with his barn-raisin' after all."

"Where's that?" asked Felver.

Dalhart spit out a fleck of tobacco. "Up north, on past the home place. Pretty good shindig, I'd think. Lots of people — women to put out the good eats, a crew of men to put up the barn in a couple of days, and then a big party and dance." Dalhart put on a smile and a wink. "But, see, the boss didn't want to go."

Percy smiled. "I hate to see you miss it, Jim. I really do. But like I told you, we don't have time for both, and I feel plumb guilty for not having a crew of women to serve pie." Percy looked at Felver. "I was lucky to get this lumber when I did. It came at just the right time, and I couldn't afford to wait. I wanted to get it all nailed together before it got hard and warped. You can see, some of it's already hard to work with."

Dalhart tipped his head up and took a comical puff on his smoke. "I should've bribed Coper not to deliver it for a couple more weeks."

Percy made a tight smile. "I'm glad you didn't."

Felver perked up at the mention of the shipping operator. "Oh, did Coper haul this in?"

"His men did," said Percy.

Dalhart sniffed. "I don't think you'll find him handling splintery lumber or wrestling kegs of nails."

Percy broke into a broad smile. "Well, now, Jim, there's another event you're missing."

"What's that?"

"Well, you know, he's having a social affair for the traveling preacher. I believe I heard it was an ice cream social, or something along that line. And you know, Jim, there's bound to be women there, too."

Dalhart laughed. "I can miss that one. I'll let Coper crank the ice cream, and I'll let the church women serve it." He took another jovial puff on his cigarette. "Gimme a ranch girl that knows how to shoot kah-oats, or even a nester girl that knows how to squirt a fly by squeezin' a cow tit."

Felver laughed. He had an image of the kind of women that Dalhart called church women, with the unfortunate Mrs. Coper in their midst, and he had to agree with Dalhart. Even a nester girl would be easier to be around.

Percy spoke again. "Well, I'm glad to know you think about something other than food. I wouldn't want you to worry about just one thing all day."

"That's for sure. There's always at least three things — somethin' to eat, somethin' to drink, and somethin' to squeeze. And not necessarily always in that order. Ain't that right, Felver?"

"I guess so." Felver glanced at Prunty, standing off by himself and grinding his boot heel into the stub of his cigarette. He wondered if Prunty enjoyed any of those things.

As the men got back into their work, Felver saw that Percy had a talent for working his men. He was efficient without being pushy, so he got plenty of work out of his men. He took all of Dalhart's comments in good humor, and he didn't seem bothered by Prunty's dour nature.

When the sun was straight overhead, about three-fourths of the floor was nailed down. Percy looked at the sun and said, "Let's see if we can finish the floor before we eat. Then, if Clarence still isn't here, we can rustle up something out of Owen's grub."

Felver sawed fast when it was his turn. He felt his arm swell with the exertion. He was hot and sweaty, hungry and thirsty. The sooner they got the floor down, the sooner they could eat. Dalhart seemed to be thinking the same, as he didn't waste a minute.

When they had all the planks cut and were waiting for Prunty to nail down the last two, Felver saw a canvas-covered wagon heading toward the camp.

"There's Clarence," said Dalhart.

Percy looked up. "He made good time."

The wagon came creaking down the slope, past the picketed horses, and into the camp. Felver saw a gray-bearded man handling the reins, presumably the same Clarence who had been taking a nap the afternoon before.

Percy spoke again. "Why don't you two help him get set up, so he can get dinner started."

Clarence climbed down from the wagon and took a few limping steps toward the building site until he stopped. Felver got his first good look at the man. He looked as if he was somewhere in his fifties, and his build was starting to go slack. His shirt and vest hung on him, and his trousers sagged beneath a belly that was starting to round out. He wore a sweat-stained brown hat with a narrow trough on the crown and with the left side of the brim turned up higher than the right. Felver thought it possible that Clarence had laid the hat on its side at one time or another and used it for a pillow.

"Well, I made it," the older man said. "I guess I'll get set up in the same place as I did on roundup."

As Dalhart and Felver walked toward the wagon, Dalhart spoke. "Just in time, Clarence. Felver and I can help you get set up."

Clarence looked at Felver. "You must be the new one."

As Dalhart made introductions, Felver got a closer look at Clarence. The older man had a purple face above the gray beard, and the whites had gone yellow around his brown eyes. He looked as if he had had a hard life, much of it by his own choice, and he did not look like a happy man.

He looked at Felver and said, "You can go ahead and dig out the fire pit." Then to Dalhart he said, "Gather up a bunch of them wood scraps, and we'll see if they can make a quick fire."

Felver found a shovel in the wagon and looked around the worn area that had obviously been a camp site before. He found the old fire pit, which was nearly full with dirt that had been shoveled back in. Jabbing the shovel into the dirt, he felt it hit something that gave a little, like buried wood, and he imagined someone had shoveled in dirt to kill a fire that had been burning when the wagon was ready to roll out. As he dug out the pit, he brought up pieces of charred firewood along with bits of charcoal and a general mixture of ashes and dirt.

"Make 'er square with a level bottom," said Clarence, who had come to stand nearby. "Just like I had 'er before."

Felver looked up and nodded.

Dalhart arrived with an armload of lumber scraps and dropped them next to the pit. "Felver says he brought us some good deer meat, Clarence."

Felver glanced at the older man to see what he would say.

Clarence spit out a gob of tobacco juice and said, "That's good. Anything is better than havin' to kill your own beef, and I didn't bring anything fresh. Just salt pork."

Felver could see Clarence's mouth as he spoke. What teeth he had were yellow and brown, and the beard around the edges was stained.

"Hurry up," said the old man. "I'm goin' to turn the wagon around and bring it closer. Then I'll have Bill put the horses out."

Felver went back to shoveling. He heard the last few blows of Prunty's hammer, and then he heard Clarence hollering about the horses.

When the pit was cleaned out, Felver found a

camp hatchet and split up some kindling. Dalhart got the fire going while Felver went to his heap of gear and dug out a hind quarter of venison. He carried it back to the wagon to Clarence, who bent over and sniffed it.

"Smells all right, for all it's kinda black around the edges. Take it to the back of the wagon and cut it into pieces about yay." With his thumb and forefinger he gave a measurement of about an inch. "You've got enough for two meals there, so you know what's for supper."

Clarence's wagon was neat and orderly. Felver found a wood-handled butcher knife and a cutting board, and he went to work cutting the meat into cubes. The fire grew hot at his back, so he moved to the other side of the end gate.

"Git back over there," said Clarence. "I need to mix my dough here."

Dalhart came back with more lumber scraps and dropped them in their place. "That's it," he said.

"Go git me a bucket of water, then, and git the coffeepot ready."

Clarence went on in that fashion, rattling out orders to everyone, including the boss. Felver imagined that some of it was for his benefit, as he was a newcomer, and he didn't mind. Besides, Clarence was getting out a meal in short order.

Clarence had parked the wagon north-south,

so a little shade was starting to show on the east side, on the other side of the wagon from the fire. When the coffeepot was resting on the coals, the meat was frying, and the biscuits were sitting in the Dutch oven waiting to go on the coals, Clarence told the men they could get out of the way now, as he needed to cook the meat and then make gravy.

Percy, Dalhart, and Felver sat in the band of shade, while Prunty stood out in the sun. As before, he had a humorless air about him, and he seemed as if he thought it was his lot in life to suffer — as if he wasn't supposed to enjoy anything. Smoking a cigarette seemed like a self-imposed punishment, just as rolling it seemed like a job he had to do.

By the time dinner was ready, the shade had crept out onto the dry grass. The men sat spaced apart as they ate their grub. Prunty, when he had dished up his plate, went back to stand in the sun.

Clarence went into one of his tirades. "For Christ's sake, Bill, come over here and sit in the shade and eat like a white man."

Prunty looked at him as if it were the first thing he had heard all day, but he said nothing.

Clarence, still standing at the end of the wagon, went on. "By Jesus, you're a fool not to get over here in the shade. I got my brains baked enough when I was your age, and by God, I learned to find my shade wherever I can get it in this weather."

93

"That's why you need a good fat woman," said Dalhart. "You'd have plenty of shade."

"Piss on you," said Clarence, looking down at Dalhart. "And don't think I haven't had my share of snatch."

Felver was startled for a second. It was the first time he had heard an older man use the word.

Dalhart smiled. "Don't get mad, Clarence. I just didn't want you to run out of shade."

Clarence poked a chunk of meat into the center of his bearded face. "Don't you worry about me."

Dalhart winked at Percy and said, "Ain't that right, Felver? Ain't that a good way to get shade?"

Felver smiled. "I don't know. The last woman I saw that could give shade like that was so pale I don't think she could last five minutes in the sun."

Dalhart laughed. "I think I saw the same one. But she's not the only punkin in the patch. I know there's some good ones out there."

"Well," said Percy, "I hope you find one."

"If I do, at least I know who to talk to if I want to get 'er shipped out this way."

Everyone but Prunty laughed at that one.

When Felver was through laughing, he found himself feeling a little guilty. "I don't know," he said, "but maybe we shouldn't be laughin' at her. From what I understand, when people get that way, it's not their fault.

Somethin' inside just goes bugs."

"I think you're right," Dalhart agreed. "I really didn't want to make fun of her personally." He paused. "But as for the shippin' agent, a joke or two in that direction might not be so cruel."

Percy looked at Felver as he said, "I gather that you know him."

Felver shrugged. "I've just bumped into him once or twice." As an afterthought he said, "But I'm not mad because I can't go to his ice cream social."

Clarence, who had taken a seat in the shade, said, "Aw, he's all right. People just don't like him 'cause he's a little uppity. But he gets the freight hauled."

Felver expected Percy to say, "His men do," but a moment of silence passed instead.

Finally Dalhart spoke. "Well, I've crossed paths with him a few times, and even if he gets the freight hauled, I don't trust him."

Percy's eyebrows went up and down, but still he said nothing.

Dalhart spoke again. "I think it's his eyes. I always heard you shouldn't trust someone whose eyes are that close together. He could look through a peep sight with both of 'em at the same time."

Felver recalled an image he had had earlier, in a conversation with Jenny — it was an image of Coper at the keyhole. He looked again at Percy, who still seemed to be making an effort not to say anything. After a moment, Felver spoke. "Well, there does seem to be something about him."

The conversation went into a stall then, until Percy spoke. "Well, Clarence, I've got to compliment you on the grub."

"Best compliment is to have seconds," said Clarence. "Like Bill there."

Felver looked up and saw Prunty moving away from the wagon with a plate of grub. The lean man went back to his previous spot in the sun and sat down this time. Felver looked back at Percy, who got up and went for a second helping. Dalhart and Clarence were eating now and not saying a thing. It was quite a crew, Felver thought. Percy had to be pretty good to steer a middle course through these others, day in and day out.

When the men went back to work, Clarence rolled out a bedroll and took a nap in the shade of the wagon. No amount of hammering seemed to wake him, even though Prunty was now cobbling together a wall as it lay flat on the new floor, where the noise echoed against the wood surface. After a couple of hours, Clarence got up and called to Felver and Dalhart, who then helped him set up a canvas fly off the end of the wagon.

"Make your jokes," he said to Dalhart, "but this is for rain and sun both."

The work crew sawed and hammered through the hot afternoon, and when they had two walls put together and lying on the ground, Percy called it a day.

The wagon cast a heavier, more solid shade than the canvas did, so the men sat there to rest for a while. As usual, Prunty kept off to himself, tending to the horses and then wandering up the stream a ways. After supper, the men moved to the other side of the wagon. The sun had gone down and the air was cooling, so the warmth and the firelight were welcome.

When it was time to call it a night, Percy asked if Felver was going to set up his tent. Felver said he didn't think he'd bother until it looked like they would need it. The men dug their bedrolls out of the wagon and found places to bed down. Clarence and Percy rolled out their beds under the canvas fly; Felver and Dalhart rolled theirs out on the other side of the fire; and Prunty moved out of the firelight, in the direction of the horses, to roll out his.

Felver wondered if Prunty felt that he had to keep an ear open for the horses, as if he had to work in his sleep as part of his continual self-punishment. Prunty was a strange one, all right, with his squinty eyes and rodent face, his lean build and pinched hat. He didn't seem to enjoy anything, not even his work, even though he worked as if he were driven by a demon.

Felver lay in his bed and looked at the stars. It was a clear, calm night, quiet except for the faint sounds of the horses moving as they grazed. Felver thought about Jenny and what she might be doing at the moment. Maybe she had just gotten off work and was gazing out of her hotel window. Maybe she had already gone to bed. That was a good thought. Felver imagined she looked pretty nice in her night things. She was a clean girl, now that he thought of it. He had known some who weren't.

He looked at the vast sky. It was hard to imagine how many stars were out there or how far away they were. He wished he knew more about the stars, as some people did.

In the morning the men rolled their beds and tossed them in the wagon. They did not loiter at breakfast, and by the time the sun was up, the thump of the hammer carried on the morning air. By midmorning they had all four walls framed, standing, and tacked together. A door opening faced east, and a window opening faced south, toward the creek.

Dalhart leaned his forearms on the sill of the window. He had rolled a cigarette and was now smoking it. Percy sat on the edge of the floor, between studs, also facing the creek. Felver sat on the ground, with the shack on his left and the creek on his right. Prunty had wandered off, to check the horses or go to the bushes.

"This is it," said Dalhart. "The window to throw it out of, if a man ever had a pot to piss in." He shifted his feet, and his boot heels made a knocking noise on the floor. "What kind of window are we goin' to put in, George?"

"I ordered a window already built, the kind that slides up and down, and I hope to hell it fits. Coper should have had it here by now, but he said not to worry, I'd get exactly what I ordered."

Dalhart tapped the ash off his cigarette. "Is this the kind with window weights?"

"No, it's not that fancy. You'll have to put a stick, or a book, or a whiskey bottle in there to keep it open."

"Uh huh." Dalhart took a pull on his cigarette.

Felver looked at Percy. "Does Coper just ship these things, or does he order them as well?"

"He does both. In this case, I ordered the lumber from a sawmill in Newcastle, and Coper is shipping it. Then I ordered the nails and hardware and window through Coper. Oh, and I ordered the shingles from the sawmill."

Felver glanced around. "I hadn't thought about it, but all I've seen so far has been lumber and nails."

Percy wrinkled his nose. "Oh, that other stuff will get here. It'll take us a while to cut all the rafters and nail the trusses together, so we've got plenty to do."

Felver glanced at the roofless skeleton of a shack. Percy was building something decent, with a window and a ridged roof. It was nice to work for someone who didn't skimp.

Along about midafternoon, the window showed up. It was delivered by none other than

Hodges and Carter, who rode in a light spring wagon pulled by two horses. They unloaded the window and set it inside the frame building. Felver thought they took a good look around, but they didn't say anything to him.

Percy asked them where the shingles and the rest of the hardware were, and they said they didn't know. He asked who delivered the two stacks of lumber, and they said they didn't know that, either.

When Hodges and Carter were gone, Felver said to Dalhart, "I didn't know those two worked for Coper."

Dalhart glanced in the direction they had taken. "Neither did I. It's the most work I've known 'em to do. Not that they did much."

For the rest of the afternoon, Felver had something to think about. He wondered why Hodges and Carter would be running a petty little errand for Coper, and he wondered if their dealings with Coper ran any deeper than casual day labor. It was possible that some of their bullying had been work carried out for the man with the close-set eyes and Vandyke beard. That could be. It didn't rule out the other motive that he had given them credit for — hot blood and a willingness to fight. Well, at least they had known enough to keep their mouths shut on this go-around. And they had given everything a good looking-over. Felver nodded. That might be why Coper sent them out all this way just to deliver a window.

Chapter Six

As Percy had said, it took plenty of time to cut the rafters, notch them for the ridgepole, and nail together the trusses. Then the men mounted the trusses on the roof and connected them with the ridgepole. As he had done with the walls, Percy lined up all the trusses with his plumb bob. Sitting at each end of a thick plank that spanned the width of the shack, Dalhart and Felver held each truss upright as Prunty, standing on the plank in the middle, nailed the truss in place.

By the time they ran the slats across the rafters, the shingles had arrived, along with assorted hardware such as hinges, bolts, and latches. Also in the load were two heavy rolls of tar paper, something Felver had not seen before. Percy explained that they would roll it out on the roof and then put the shingles over it.

The shipment arrived just before noon dinner, and the men were looking over the goods.

"You're buildin' a regular house here, aren't you?" said Dalhart, rubbing at a smudge of tar between his right thumb and forefinger.

"I want to make it livable," said Percy. "I might have someone stay here who's got a wife."

Dalhart looked at Prunty, who was working the bolt on a gate latch. Dalhart opened his eyes wide and gazed at Felver.

Felver pursed his lips and said nothing. Then he recalled the two men who had delivered the materials. "Who were those two freighters?" he asked.

"Just a couple of Coper's men," said Dalhart, who seemed to know everyone. "He's got half a dozen of 'em."

"They look a little more likely than the two that delivered the window."

Dalhart laughed. "Oh, yeah. These two today are the real thing. The two of them could lift a piano."

After dinner, Felver and Dalhart built a ladder while Prunty and the boss rolled out the tar paper and tacked it down. Then the four of them started the roofing. Felver carried the shingles up the ladder, Dalhart set them out in small stacks, Percy sorted them for width, and Prunty kept up a steady pounding as he nailed the shingles in place. After a few rows were down, the crew got into a rhythm. Felver was happy, even though each bundle of shingles bit into his shoulder as he went up the ladder. Dalhart was cheerful as he clumped his boot heels across the new roof. The boss was feeding shingles like fat scraps to a hungry dog, and Prunty bent his lean frame to the work.

Dalhart was singing now:

Have your silver dollars ready
When you go to Diamond Lil's —
Leave your whisperin' change at home,
*   boys —*
She don't take no dollar bills.

On they worked, through the hot afternoon. From time to time, Felver glanced at Clarence, who slept in the shade of the wagon and snored with his mouth open. This was the fourth day of the job, and the cook had taken his nap every afternoon. No amount of hammering or singing showed any effect on him.

In the late afternoon, as Felver was clearing the top of the ladder with a bundle of shingles on his shoulder, he saw Prunty lose his temper. All of a sudden the hammering came to a stop, and Prunty stood up, swearing about a sonofabitch, and threw the hammer down with a furious stroke. The hammer bounced off a slat and almost clipped Percy in the nose as it flew off into the air. Prunty was moving his left hand up and down, so Felver figured he must have mashed a finger.

"It's too damn hot up here on this tar paper," said the boss. "Let's all go down and cool off in the shade for a while."

There was plenty of shade now, with both sides of the roof papered over. When Felver came back with the hammer, Percy was sitting in the doorway. Dalhart was squatted in his style, rolling a cigarette, and even Prunty was sitting in the shade, rolling a cigarette with his left forefinger sticking up. Felver set the hammer on the floor next to the boss, and then he sat down on the ground and rested his back against the framed wall.

"We're makin' good time," said the boss. "If we finish roofing this one side, we can call it good for today."

After a rest, they went back to work and got into the rhythm again. When Felver had brought up enough shingles to finish the day's work, he lent a hand at laying them out. When the crew came to the ridge, he went down for the saw and brought it up.

Prunty nailed the last two courses of shingles so that the thin ends of both rows stuck over the ridge together. Now he was sawing them off as the other three men watched.

"You know," said Dalhart, "them real roofers, they've got a special hatchet for this kind of work. The head's square so it doesn't slip off the nail so easy, and the other side's got a hatchet blade so they can just chop off each shingle."

Prunty jammed the saw down and broke it loose from the cut he was making, popping off a few fragments of wood shingle. For a moment it looked as if he was going to fling the saw as he had done to the hammer, but then he put it back into place before he looked up, squinting at Dalhart. His gopher teeth showed as he said, "The real roofers can fook each other, and you too, for all I care."

Dalhart put his hands on his hips. "Don't get mad, Bill. I was just tryin' to cheer things up."

"You always do." Prunty wiggled the saw blade and went back to cutting.

When the day's work was done, three of the men sat in the shade of the wagon while Prunty went to take care of the horses. He gave the impression that the horses were his domain, and no one seemed willing to interfere, so Felver let him take care of his two as well, as if the men were on roundup together and Prunty was the wrangler.

Felver had noticed that Prunty had his own intricate system of pasturing the horses. One pair he hobbled together — a wagon horse and a saddle horse. With another horse, he used a picket rope and a single hobble. The rest of his boss's horses he hobbled individually, while he picketed Felver's horses as requested, with a simple rope from the halter to the picket pin.

When Prunty had taken the horses to water and was setting them out for the evening, Felver made a casual remark to Dalhart about Prunty's system of hobbling.

Clarence, who was at the tailgate mixing dough, spoke up. "You've never really had to hobble animals until you've had to hobble a string of Army mules."

"Oh," said Felver, who was learning to humor Clarence, "were you in the Army?"

"You damn right I was, and it wasn't so easy

then. You didn't go for wood or water without a gun. Why, I was at Fort Laramie when Portugee Phillips rode in with the news of the Fetterman massacre." He walked out a few yards and spit tobacco juice. "That's been over twenty-five years ago."

Dalhart set his high-crowned hat on the ground, underside up. "What year was it?"

"He rode in on Christmas night of 1866. Probably before either of you was born. So how long has that been?"

Dalhart showed his teeth in a smile. "Almost twenty-eight years. I was a little baby then, Clarence, pullin' at the slats in my crib."

"I wasn't born till the next year," said Felver.

"It was a damn sight different, I'll tell you that. The country was young then, before all these latecomers roo-eened it."

Dalhart nodded, as if he had heard it before.

Felver imagined it was a favorite theme for Clarence, who was playing on it again for a new audience. Felver wondered if Clarence had heard the same song from the old-timers twenty-five years earlier — the trappers and hunters, who said the wagon trains and the railroad had ruined the country. Felver glanced at Percy, who would be one of the latecomers, and then he looked at Clarence.

Percy, who had also taken off his hat, looked normal and harmless in his brown hair, tanned face, and brown beard. He lifted his look at Clarence as he spoke. "A man has a right to take a chance at it. I hope I'm not ruinin' anything."

Felver sensed that Clarence had a glimmering of who paid his wages.

"The cattlemen ain't so bad," said the cook. "It's the damn wheat farmers. You go back to the time I was talkin' about, and there wasn't a tumbleweed in the country. It's a fact. Then the damn wheat farmers came, and they ripped up the ground wherever they put down a claim, and now you've got tumbleweeds till hell won't have 'em. It's a fact. The tumbleweeds came with the wheat farmers. And now they're everywhere."

Dalhart had finished rolling a cigarette. He paused before lighting it and said, "What did the ranches bring in, besides horses and cattle and a few women?"

"Not a hell of a lot," Clarence answered. "Maybe a few Chinamen for cooks and a few Mexicans and Nagurs for cowpunchers. I remember a time when everyone was white, except for the Indians, and the Army was workin' on that."

Felver bit his lip. He was developing a distaste for Clarence's talk, and he didn't feel like humoring the old man anymore. He stood up and said, "I could probably make myself useful and go pick up some kindling. We got a lot of scraps out of the shingles."

Dalhart got up and put on his hat. "I suppose I could help."

When they were on the far side of the building, Felver asked Dalhart where Clarence was from.

"I don't know," answered the Texan. "I believe it was somewhere like Kansas or Missouri, but it was so long ago it probably doesn't matter."

Felver shrugged. He knew a lot of men didn't care to talk about where they were from. "Well, he seems stuck in the past, doesn't he? Or at least in what he thinks the past was like."

"Oh, yeh," said Dalhart. "It's Army this and Army that. You wonder if he likes to go back to that time because things are so piss poor for him now."

Felver thought of the purple face, yellow teeth, and slumping build. It probably didn't happen overnight, but at some point, Clarence must have looked back and decided that things used to be better. "I suppose so," he said.

They each brought in a small armload of kindling, which they laid on the ground next to the woodpile.

Clarence glanced at the stack and said, "I'm gonna need some firewood before long. Why don't you boys go up the creek and see about gettin' some?"

Felver looked at Dalhart, who nodded and picked up the ax. The first clump of trees, just west of camp, had no deadfall. Felver imagined it had been picked clean for the campfire during roundup. They walked upstream toward the next little bunch of trees, and just before they reached the trees, Dalhart stopped.

"What is it?" Felver asked, stopping along with him.

Dalhart pointed with his free right hand. "Looks like someone buried somethin' here, not too long ago."

Felver gave an arched look, and he and Dalhart walked over to the little mound of dirt, about two feet by four. "Sure enough looks like it," he said. "I think I'll go back for a shovel. This is a little close not to look into it."

Dalhart nodded. "I'd say so. I'll go ahead and round up some wood until you get back."

Felver went back to camp and told Percy what they had found. The boss put on his hat and walked with Felver to the place where the mound was. Dalhart met them and dropped a few pieces of firewood and the ax.

Felver started digging, and before long he felt the shovel hit something that had some give to it. He punched around with the shovel and felt more solid resistance in some places than in others. He shoveled out some more dirt, and before long he struck the head and horns of a cow. Next he uncovered the four lower legs, detached, and with a little more digging he unearthed a hide, doubled over.

"Sure enough someone butchered a beef," said Dalhart.

"Looks like it," Percy agreed. "You might as well pull that hide out so we can have a look at it, although I'd bet it's got the brand cut out of it."

Felver dug a little more, then hooked the blade of the shovel into the fold of the hide, and gave a pull. It came loose but did not lift out. Setting the shovel aside and kneeling, he said to Dalhart, "Give me a hand here, would you?"

Together they pulled the hide out of its grave and flopped it over once and then twice to spread it out. Felver was not surprised to see a gaping six-inch hole where a brand would have been.

"Just what we expected," he said.

"Well, go ahead and cover it back up," said Percy. "I don't like someone doing this on our place, but there's not much we can do about it."

Dalhart sniffed. "Probably some poor nester that needed the meat." He bent to help Felver fold the hide back into a heap.

"It's common enough," said Percy. "No one likes to eat his own beef if he doesn't have to. I just wish they'd do it out on the open range, and be careful about it."

Felver dug out some more dirt to make sure everything would fit back in. He scooted the hide back into the hole, and after that the head and hooves. Then, working the shovel sideways, he scraped dirt back over the remnants.

"Let me tramp 'er down," said Dalhart.

Felver stood back and rested on the shovel as

Dalhart did a side-step back and forth across the loose dirt.

"I'll see you back in camp," said Percy. "Thanks for letting me know about this." He frowned and said, "Too bad they had to waste the hide."

By suppertime, Felver had given enough thought to their discovery that he came to agree with Dalhart. It must have been someone else who lived out on the range. His first impulse was to run through a list of likely suspects that he knew, which included Hodges and Carter, Heid, and McNair. But those were just the loafers he knew, and he doubted that any of them was energetic enough to butcher a beef and haul it away. He figured there were dozens of people out this way or passing through, any of whom might have more use for a beef than the two pair of idlers did.

Nevertheless, when supper was ended and the men sat by the fire, Felver asked Dalhart what he thought about McNair and Heid.

"I don't know much at all about that fella with the funny cap. He's been around for a couple of months, and as near as I know, he hasn't done a lick of work."

Felver nodded. "That's about how I saw him, from the one time I met him. How about the other one?"

"Oh, Brownie Junior? I don't think you'll see him work, either."

"How does he manage that?"

Dalhart picked his teeth. "I guess he just leeches off of Coper. That's what I've heard. He doesn't do a bit of work, from what I hear, and when he needs money, he squeezes it from Coper. Damnedest thing, really."

"Is he from St. Louis?"

"I believe so. I think he followed Coper out here."

"Do you think they're related?"

"Nah, not really. We just call him Junior because he wears a brown suit like Coper and leeches off him like a ne'er-do-well son."

Felver laughed. "He says he's a photographer."

Dalhart's teeth gleamed in the firelight. "He might be, but he hasn't done much of it here."

Felver was about to tell what he had heard from Heid, about wanting to have his equipment shipped out, but then he thought of something that didn't fit. If Heid could squeeze Coper whenever he wanted, why didn't he have him ship the equipment? He couldn't recall Heid saying anything that actually expressed contempt, but he had a general impression that Heid sneered at Coper even as he associated with him. Felver remembered Coper's remark about hearing from Heid about Felver seeing Jenny. There seemed to be a level of confidence there — unless Coper had seen it himself and was passing off his knowledge as secondhand information. Hell, thought Felver, it could be anything. Maybe there was no equipment.

Maybe there was, and Heid didn't want Coper to touch it. Maybe Heid had some level of confidence with Coper and then laughed as he drank up his money. Whatever the case, Heid must have his hooks into Coper one way or another.

"Beats all, doesn't it?" came Dalhart's voice.

"What's that?"

"How a fella like Coper can afford to dole out money to a loafer like Heid, and pay that other shiftless pair to deliver a window."

Percy spoke up. "He knows how to make money, you know."

"I suppose," said Dalhart, "but he doesn't spend it very smart." Then he looked at Felver and laughed. "But who does?"

The next day, the men were back on the roof to cover the south side. They got into the swing of it again and had the roof done by dinnertime. In the afternoon they started putting on the bat-and-board exterior. The first lumber pile was gone now, and the second one was going down. Felver tried to imagine what the remaining lumber would be used for, once they finished the shack.

"Do you plan to build a stable or shed?" he asked, as the men sat in the shade of the building at the end of the day.

"Just a little one," said Percy. "And a corral for horses."

"A couple or three more days, maybe?"

"I hope it's no more than that, but we'll see."

Dalhart joined in. "I'm just glad we finished with the roof. That was the worst part, with the heat of the tarpaper and the glare of the shingles."

"None of it's easy," said Prunty, in his strained voice.

"No, it isn't," said the boss, "but we're making good time."

They finished the outside walls by noon the next day. The four of them measured, cut, and nailed together a front door in half an hour after dinner, and then Percy put Dalhart and Felver to digging holes for the corner posts of the shed while he and Prunty hung the window and door.

Dalhart, unlike most Texans who came up the trail, would at least work with a shovel even if he wasn't very handy at it. He spent a lot of time sticking and jabbing at the first posthole while Felver carried over the four posts. Felver then took the shovel and dug the next two holes while Dalhart carried the cross pieces and the rafters. Then they switched again, with Dalhart digging the last hole while Felver carried more lumber.

The lumber pile was east of the wagon, while the shack was west of it and a little south. Felver and Dalhart were laying out the shed straight west of the house. It would be three-sided, with the open side facing the creek and away from the bad weather. The corral would run out from the shed on its open side about ten yards, with a gate on the east. It all looked simple enough, even if it called for a dozen more postholes for the corral.

Percy with his plumb bob and Prunty with the mattock handle tamped in the four corner posts for the shed. Prunty seemed to have come out of the worst part of his bad humor, but he still squinted and grimaced and showed his gopher teeth. Felver dug postholes for the corral while Dalhart carried posts and rails. Generally, a peaceful atmosphere prevailed. For the first time in days, no hammer pounding carried on the air. Clarence took his nap as always, and the spirit moved Dalhart to sing again:

You can have your fried bacon and sausage,
The best that a farm can produce —
But give me a fat-cracklin' gander,
For there's nothing like roasting a goose.
You can have your fine wines
    and Scotch whiskey,
Your gin and your grenadine juice —
Just give me a bottle of red-eye,
To drink while I'm roasting my goose.
You can have all the lobster and codfish,
Your steaks from the elk and the moose —
For me it's a far greater pleasure
To savor a fat roasted goose.
And after the banquet is over,
My napkin will be hanging loose.
My chin will be shiny and greasy,
For there's nothing like roasting a goose.

He sang the whole song twice, drawing out the last refrain in a loud voice. Prunty looked over his shoulder and gave a cross look, but Percy had a smile on his face. Why not? thought Felver. The work was moving along, and most of the workers were happy. If Prunty didn't like to hear about other people's pleasures, much less enjoy them himself, that was too bad. Tomorrow he could go back to pounding nails.

That night, Felver lay in his bed and looked at the stars. It had been almost a week since he had seen Jenny, and it looked as if he would be free of this job in a few more days. He didn't mind the job; he just wanted a chance to ride into town and see a girl he liked. There were other things in town, too, like cold beer, but he could wait for that. It would be nice to see Jenny, though, as soon as he could.

He wondered how much there was to know about the stars — or even the moon, for that matter. The night was peaceful now, with no wind and no noise by man or beast. Off in the towns and cities, people would be carrying on, drinking and laughing and singing. That was all right. This was a good place to be tonight, if he didn't have much choice anyway. He could lie here and look at the stars and think of a girl as the refrain of Dalhart's song ran through his mind.

Chapter Seven

They put up the shed in one day and the corral in another. The venison ran out, and Clarence took to serving fried salt pork at every meal, along with his usual beans and biscuits. He said it wasn't worth the trouble of killing more meat until they got back to the ranch. Felver ate his grub and told himself to like it, even if it had a bit more salt, sand, and ashes than he cared for. He worked a total of eight days for George Percy, who paid him ten dollars wages and a dollar bonus, all in silver.

"Come out and see us sometime," he said. "If you're still around at fall roundup time, we could use a hand."

Felver thanked him, said good-bye to the others, and rode leading his packhorse. He didn't have a definite plan for what he was going to do next, but he knew he wanted to go see Jenny, so he headed back to his previous campsite across from Red Bluff.

Once there, he pitched his camp as he had before, using the same tent poles. It didn't look as if anyone had camped there or even stayed long, as there was still a pile of firewood where he had left it. He looked through his gear to check on his provisions, which he hadn't touched in his stay at Percy's work camp. All he had was dry food — flour, salt, baking powder, coffee, rice, and beans. He wasn't in any hurry to eat more bacon or salt pork right away, and he didn't want to hunt another animal just yet. The more he thought about it, the more he liked the idea of a juicy beefsteak and a plate of potatoes. It was better to buy provisions on a full stomach anyway, he thought.

He looked overhead and saw the sun at high noon. He could just ride into town now. Looking out at the horses, he saw the chestnut. He could have the saddle back on in a couple of minutes and be on his way.

As he was saddling the horse, he was not surprised to see Hodges and Carter riding in from the northeast. They had their six-guns out in view as usual, and they rode into his camp without stopping or calling out.

"Thought you'd be gone by now," said Hodges.

Felver gave the two of them a sideways look as he pulled the cinch. "I had a job. Working for wages."

Carter spoke next. "Well, it looks like you don't now. Why don't you just move along, like you ought to?"

Felver looked at Carter's tight face and saw the taunt there once again. "Why don't you get it through your thick head that I go or stay as I please?"

Carter narrowed his eyes so they looked like pig eyes. "You really are a smart-mouthed little whoremonger, aren't you?"

Felver could feel his pulse jump. He made himself remember what he had thought before, that Carter was good at making a man want to fight. "Think what you want," he said.

Hodges said, "Well, I think the same, and I don't like it."

Felver looked at the thick lips and droopy eyes, and he thought he'd like to plant a fist there. But he kept control and said, "You don't have to like it."

"No," said Carter, still pushing. "But we don't have to put up with it, either."

Felver looked at the high boots and wrist cuffs and then the hard face again. "Did Coper send you out here?"

"Nobody sent us," Carter answered. "We were just in the neighborhood, and we didn't think we'd be interruptin' your bath."

"Yeah," said Hodges. "We smelled something, so we thought we'd ride in and see what it was."

"Well, I guess you got that done, then."

"You'll guess again before long," said Carter.

Felver appreciated the way the two upstarts worked their taunts back and forth. He could also see that they knew they wouldn't get him to fight this time, either. The moment for that had passed. He said nothing as he let silence hang in the air.

Finally Hodges said, "Let's go." He reined his horse around and kicked it into a lope. Carter gave one last, hard look with his pig eyes and then followed his partner.

Felver watched them ride away as he hooked up the back cinch and tightened it. They really were a shiftless pair, and they could give trouble yet. He glanced at the brown pack-horse, still out on picket, and decided to put it in the livery stable for a few days. He had left it here alone a few times already, and he didn't want to push his luck.

He rubbed his hand on his jaw and realized he could use a bath and a shave. He shouldn't be in such a hurry to go to town. If it was obvious to Hodges and Carter that he needed cleaning up, it would be obvious to anyone in town as well. He looked at the creek and frowned. There wasn't a pool big enough to bathe in, and he didn't want to take the time to gather rocks and build a little dam. He rubbed his jaw again, then turned his nose to his shoulder and smelled himself. What he really needed was a dunk in a real bathtub, and he thought a regular shave wouldn't hurt. He dug into his gear in the tent and picked out a clean shirt, clean socks, and clean underwear, then wrapped the clothes in his slicker.

As he tied the bundle onto the back of his saddle, he thought about how he would do things. He couldn't do everything at once, and if he decided to take a bath first, then he would have to hurry through his bath and still eat a late dinner. He turned down the corners of his mouth. He was hungry already. Jenny wouldn't have time to talk until she got off work anyway, and by then he'd be clean. He nodded as he pulled the saddle strings tight on the bundle. The little bonus he had received would cover the shave and bath and then some.

Once in town, he left the horse at the stable and went to the café. Not much had changed. The man with the cigar still sat in his place at the cash box, and the heavy-boned woman still perspired and breathed hard. Felver was anxious to see Jenny, but he felt a small relief at not having her see him before he got cleaned up. He ordered his steak and potatoes and then sat back to drink his coffee.

When his meal came, he took his time and enjoyed it. For dessert he had pie made from dried peaches, and he savored that as well. He had still not caught a glance of Jenny when he was done eating. He asked for her, and the woman in the greasy braid told him she was in the kitchen. Felver thought that was good enough, as he wasn't highly presentable, so he asked the woman to relay a message that he would drop in later. He paid his bill and walked out into the bright afternoon.

After fetching his clean clothes from the saddle, he walked across the street to the barbershop. There he leaned back in a padded chair while the barber lathered and shaved him. After that he went to the back, where he shucked his dirty clothes and climbed into an oblong tin tub of warm water. The shave had been soothing, but this was even more so. He was glad he had chosen not to hurry through this part, even if it meant taking a bath on a full stomach. He felt full as a pup, but that was all right. He was going to get good and clean, and he hoped he got close enough to Jenny for her to appreciate it.

Back out in the sunlight an hour later, he felt spanking clean as he tied the slicker with the old clothes onto the back of the saddle. He looked around him, and even though he didn't see anyone watching him, he had the sense that someone saw him. Maybe it was Coper, or the clerk in the mercantile, or some other small-town busybody. He shrugged. He couldn't worry about someone else knowing where he put his dirty laundry.

The afternoon had crept along somewhat, and the sun was starting to slip. Felver thought it was late enough in the day for a respectable fellow like himself to have a drink. To avoid walking past the café and being tempted to peek in, he walked around the back of his horse and stepped up onto the sidewalk in front of the Blue Horse Saloon.

Once inside, he looked into a dark corner, closed his eyes for a few seconds, and opened them again. There was only one other patron in the bar, and that was McNair, easily identified by the short-billed cap. He was seated at a table a little ways from the bar, and he was facing the door. He greeted Felver with a look of recognition and a wave.

Felver ordered a mug of beer, and it tasted good. He would have liked to drink it by himself and appreciate this pleasure he had missed for well over a week, but he thought it would look unsociable if he didn't join McNair. He took another sip and then went to McNair's table, where he was invited to sit down.

McNair looked the same as before, generally unshaven and unwashed, with a shady, sunken look to his eyes. His whole countenance had an even texture to it, as if he were covered in a film of dry grime that had not been disturbed by sun, wind, or water. He was drinking whiskey, as before, and he had what looked like the same soggy-ended cigarette in his mouth. It occurred to Felver that a person could believe McNair had not left the Blue Horse Saloon and did not exist apart from it.

"What's in the wind?" Felver asked as he settled into his seat.

McNair shook his head. "Nothin' new that I know of. And yourself?"

"About the same."

"Hadn't seen you for a while. Thought maybe you'd gone off on a packin' trip."

Felver paused as he took a sip of beer. He was not disappointed that he wasn't more important, but he had thought Hodges and Carter might have contributed their knowledge to the general fund of town gossip. "No," he said. "I've just been out of town a ways, workin'. I

123

just today got back and got cleaned up."

"Oh."

Felver imagined it would take a more delicate man than McNair to be sensitive to comments about work and hygiene, and he imagined the short answer to be an invitation to give more details. "I've been workin' for a fella named George Percy, straight west of here about six miles."

"Oh, what's he been doin' there?"

Felver caught himself frowning. Percy had had enough lumber and other materials shipped out to the place that McNair should have picked up something out of the barroom banter, even if it didn't include Felver's whereabouts. He thought about saying they had been building a bank, but he went ahead and treated the question seriously. "We built a line shack, a little stable, and a corral."

"Oh," said McNair. The sunken eyes shifted and then settled on his drink. He looked up and said, "I thought his place would be farther north."

"It is. This is a different place. I understand it's a place that his hired man Prunty filed on."

McNair's face showed for the first time that he was hearing something new. "Oh, him. The jolly cowboy."

Felver smiled as he recalled Prunty. "Yeah."

"Is that fallin'-down drunk Clarence still the cook?"

"Yes, he is. He was pretty sober all the time I was there."

McNair spit tobacco from the end of his cigarette. "I've never seen him that way in town. Every time I've seen him, he couldn't find his ass with both hands."

Felver took a sip on his beer. "I could believe that."

McNair rotated his whiskey glass with his right hand, and without raising his eyes he said, "They're quite a bunch. That fella Percy, he wants to be a big bastard, doesn't he?"

Felver raised his eyebrows. "Not so much that I noticed."

A gleam came into McNair's primitive-looking face. "A damn land-grabber is what he is. He's just like the rest, only a little ways behind 'em yet. Just sackin' it up, meanwhile he pinches out a dollar a day to the ones that are really makin' it for him." McNair seemed to be working himself into a bit of a temper, as fire had come into his eyes. He took a pull on his cigarette and then held it out and pointed it at Felver. "I wouldn't work for him. Not for him or any of the others."

"Work's work," said Felver. "He treated me all right."

McNair had his head up now as he put the cigarette back in his mouth. "You watch. In a coupla years he'll be right in there with the rest of 'em, steppin' on the little man as he grabs up more. They're all the same. And they wonder why someone takes a crack at 'em when they can."

Felver recalled the hide with the brand cut out. He still couldn't imagine McNair going to the trouble of going out onto the prairie and butchering a beef, much less digging a hole to hide the evidence. He took McNair's comment to be a broad endorsement of anyone who did put himself out to filch from the land barons.

Felver thought about his answer and phrased it with care. "I didn't really hear any talk about rustlin' or anything like that."

"Nah, but you couldn't blame someone if they did."

Felver didn't have an answer to the comment, or at least not an answer that he thought had any purpose at the moment. He stared at the table, noticing McNair's fingers and thumb, yellow-stained from holding so many cigarettes. Finally he thought of something to say. "Where's our friend Heid today?"

McNair gave a bob to his heavy-browed head as he made an openmouthed smile. "I'd say he's probably still sleepin', but I imagine he's up by now. He usually drags in here at about this time."

McNair turned out to be correct, for it was only a matter of minutes until Heid came into the saloon. He looked as he did before — as if he had bathed and shaved and put on clean clothes a couple of days before and had then taken a long train ride. He took a seat at McNair's right, keeping his back to the wall and a more or less equal distance between himself and his two companions.

He gave Felver a somber nod, suggesting ex-aggerated seriousness, and took out his curved-stem pipe. "What say?" he chirped.

"Not much," said Felver. "Just got in from workin' for George Percy for a week or so."

"Oh, uh-huh." Heid's mustache went up and down as he wiggled his nose. "All done?"

"Yep." Felver grinned and looked at McNair. "Came in to squander my new wealth."

Heid began to stuff his pipe. "You came to the right place," he said, looking up. "They accept coin of the realm here."

"I noticed. That's why I came back."

Heid struck a match and cupped it over his pipe, casting a shadow on his face as he puffed a cloud of smoke. "A wise decision. I almost thought you'd come back to see some-one."

Felver's stomach tightened. "No one we'd mention here."

Heid shook out his match and tossed it on the floor. "Sorry," he said. "I forgot my man-ners. It's the company I keep." He looked at McNair. "I do say, Link, I thought you'd have a bottle on the table when I got here."

McNair wagged his head in what passed for slyness. "He knows to bring one now."

Heid raised his hand at the barkeep, who made short work of bringing over a bottle and another glass.

Felver waited until Heid had poured a drink.

Then he tried out a comment. "I met a couple of Coper's men."

"I don't doubt it. He sent a few out there."

Felver found it interesting that Heid was not pretending to know nothing about Percy's job. "These two were named Hodges and Carter."

"Really?" said Heid, looking at his drink. "What do they do for him?"

"I don't know what all. They were delivering a window that day."

"Rare moment for them, I'd say, if it was something that could be called work."

Felver smiled. "It wasn't a very big window."

McNair and Heid both laughed, and Felver laughed with them. The conversation went on to lighter, or at least less personal, topics such as the use of paper money, the villainy of the railroad tycoons, and the need for more women in the outposts of civilization. Felver expected another whorehouse joke from McNair, but none came forth. Felver did not foresee enough pleasure in a second beer, so when he sipped the last of his mug, he got up and took his leave.

Felver got back to the café at a good time, when work had slowed down and the man with the cigar had disappeared for a while. After being served coffee, Felver mentioned to the waitress that he had come back to see if Jenny had a free moment. The heavy woman walked back to the kitchen.

Felver's pulse quickened as Jenny came out

of the kitchen. She was wearing a white apron over her gray dress and looked as if she'd had a good steaming in the kitchen, but she still looked fine to him. Her face was relaxed in a smile as she walked his way and came to a stop at his table.

"I'm glad you came back," she said. "Nell said you came by earlier."

"Why don't you sit down?"

She brushed a stray hair out of her eyes. "I really shouldn't." She looked around and then back at him. "Are you going to be in town for long?"

"I could wait around till you get off work, if you'd like me to."

"That would be good." Her blue eyes sparkled.

"I can wait on the bench outside, like before."

"Okay," she said. "I'll see you then."

Felver watched her walk back to the kitchen. She looked good — maybe a little bedraggled, but that was no wonder. He probably looked like that every day when he worked for Percy. She looked more familiar to him now, or more like his own kind, than when he had first met her, and he realized that how she looked depended on how he saw her. Thinking back a few minutes, he liked the way he had felt when he first saw her walking out of the kitchen.

After drinking two cups of coffee, he still had plenty of time to kill. He chose not to go back into the Blue Horse Saloon, where he imagined Heid and McNair were well settled into their daily routine. He untied his horse, walked him down the street for a drink of water, and walked him back to the same spot where he had been hitched earlier.

Felver decided not to sit on the bench just yet, as customers were beginning to show up for supper. Looking up and down the street, he thought he might take another look at the saloon where he had seen Hodges and Carter. He saw now that it was called the Doubloon, and when he paused at the doorway he saw that Hodges and Carter were not among the half-dozen men who stood at the bar. Nobody sat at the tables yet.

Inside, Felver took his place at the bar and asked for a beer. While he waited, he observed a painting behind the bar. It featured a pirate on the deck of a ship with masts and sails and railing. The pirate wore a three-cornered hat and a jacket with ornamental cuffs. He also had a sharp black beard, and with one foot up on a spool of rope, he cut a dashing pose as he peered through a spyglass. In the distance was another ship, presumably ripe for the looting. The painting was labeled *Pieces of Eight*.

The beer came, and Felver sipped. It wasn't as cold as the beer in the Blue Horse Saloon, but it was worth drinking nevertheless. He looked around at the other men. They were all working-class men, in hats and boots, with the suntanned, windblown look that came to freighters, ditch graders, and range riders. No one paid him any attention, and as there was no mirror, just the painting, it was easy to drink his beer and mind his own business.

He drank the beer slowly, so the last couple of swallows were warm. A glance toward the open doorway told him it was still light outside, but he wasn't having much enjoyment in the Doubloon, so he walked out onto the sidewalk.

The street was quiet, with no wagons or coaches. Horses stood at the hitch racks, and the sunlight was slanting down yellow with a shade of pink. He decided it was late enough to go sit on the bench.

Daylight faded, and dusk settled on the little town. Customers came out of the café one or two at a time and hardly gave him a glance. He heard someone latch the door, and after that the door was silent. He sat in the gathering dark for another half hour, until he heard the latch again. He stood up, and he saw her light features emerge from the doorway as she closed the door behind her.

"Thanks for waiting," she said.

"Glad to."

"It's been a while, hasn't it?"

"Over a week." He fell in beside her as they walked along the sidewalk.

"I thought about you," she said.

"Oh, I did, too. I thought about you every night when I looked up at the stars."

"How did it go with your job?"

"Oh, fine. It finished up yesterday, so today I moved back to my old camp."

"That's good." She was quiet for a couple of paces until she looked at him and said, "I was wondering what you were going to do next — you know, if you were going to leave."

He looked at her and smiled. "I really don't have anything planned. I just wanted to see you, and — I guess that was as far as I had thought."

They walked on, skirting the big patches of light and crossing the small ones. When they drew near to her hotel, he said, "I hope you don't have to go in right away."

"Not really," she said. "But I don't know what else there is to do."

He shrugged. "We could go out to my camp. It's not that far. We could sit around and talk, and slap mosquitoes."

She let out a sigh. "I'm tired, and I don't know if I want to walk that far."

"You can ride."

She looked down at her dress. "Not like this. And it wouldn't look good if I went in and changed clothes and came back out."

He looked at her feet, as if there were an answer there. He could go get the other horse at the livery stable, but that wouldn't look good, either, especially if he wanted to bring it back and leave it off later. And there was still the problem of how she would ride.

"Look," he said, "we can walk out to the

edge of town, and then you can get up and ride behind me. It'll be dark, and no one will see you. Not even me."

She hesitated for a long minute and then said, "Well, I guess we could give it a try."

"Sure." He patted her shoulder. "There'll be nothin' to it."

She laughed. "I've heard that before."

He felt a twinge of embarrassment until he thought to say, "Not from me."

They walked out beyond the edge of town and came to a stop.

"Let me get on first," he said. He swung into the saddle, and then he drew his left foot from the stirrup and moved the foot in front of the stirrup. "Here," he said. "I've got the stirrup free for you. Just put your foot in it, and grab my belt or the back of the saddle, and pull yourself on."

At the edge of his vision he saw a pale gleam as she lifted her foot to the stirrup.

"What do I do now?" she asked. "I need my hands to hold up my dress."

Forcing himself to look straight ahead, he said, "Maybe you can tuck it under your chin or something."

He didn't see exactly how she did it, but he heard a rustle of cloth and felt her pull herself on board.

"What's this?" she asked.

"Oh, that's just my dirty clothes. I cleaned up in town."

He heard her slap her leg, and then she said, "You weren't just joking about the mosquitoes."

"Don't worry," he said. "We'll be there in no time."

At camp, he gave her a blanket to cover up with, more for the mosquitoes than the temperature, although the night air was cooling. He got a fire going with some of the firewood left over from his first camp, and soon enough the campsite was bright and cheery.

He sat down next to her and said, "This is nice enough. No one to bother us."

She let out a sigh. "It's good for a change. I got to feelin' like I was in jail. Every night I just go from work to my room, and that's it."

"It's hard for a girl to do anything in a little town like this, isn't it?"

"I guess. I don't even want to walk out on the street. I'm sure there's always someone to see what I do or where I go."

Felver winked. "We gave 'em the slip this time, though."

She laughed. "I hope so, because I wasn't very ladylike gettin' up on that horse."

He laughed along with her. He wondered what she looked like with her dress up, and all he could imagine was something white and shapely. Brushing the thought away, he said, "I could make coffee if you'd like some."

She shook her head. "I don't care for any, thanks."

He poked at the fire with a stick. "What do you think?"

"I already answered that one."

"Oh, that's right." After a moment's thought, he said, "I guess I was wonderin' what you thought since we saw each other last."

"Well, I missed you."

"Well, yeah, I did too." After a pause he said, "Anything else?"

She was looking at the fire. "Oh, maybe."

"For instance —"

"For instance, I wonder what you think of me."

"Oh, I think you're nice."

She looked at him. "That doesn't mean anything in particular."

"Well, I think you're . . . I don't know . . . nice. I like to be around you. I always want to see you again, and when I see you I feel good."

"What else?"

He looked at the fire. "Well, I guess I've thought about how I'd like to kiss you again."

"Is that all?"

He couldn't bring his gaze up to meet hers. "Well, I don't know. I mean, there's more than that, of course, but —"

"That's not what I mean."

He looked at her now. "What do you mean, then?"

She had a serious look in her eyes. "I mean that after you kiss me, will you still care about me?"

He shrugged. "Well, one kiss leads to another."

"Oh, Owen, are you trying to be stupid?"

He wanted to take her hand, but everything was under the blanket, so he laid his hand on top of what he was sure was her arm. "No, I'm not. I just don't know what you mean."

Her face was still serious, but it was soft in the firelight. "I mean, is that all you care about, the kissing?"

He bit his lower lip. "Well, no, not at all. Why?"

She lowered her gaze. "Because men can be that way."

He put his hand under her chin, and she looked at him again. He felt more sure of himself now that he knew what they were talking about. Her eyes looked soft now, and he felt soft inside as he said, "I sure hope you don't think I'm that way."

She shook her head slowly, and his hand fell away. Everything seemed all right now. They moved toward each other, sitting by the campfire, and they met in a kiss. It was a soft, moist kiss that almost ended and then continued.

He felt awkward, sitting in his twisted position with her wrapped up in the blanket. "There's got to be a more comfortable way," he said.

They both stood up, and he took her in his arms and held her to him. He felt her breasts press against him as they kissed again.

He locked his hands around her waist as they ended the kiss and looked into each other's eyes. He closed his eyes and held his head next to hers, then drew back and met her for a couple of short kisses.

Then they had a long kiss again, and this time he felt all of her body against his, and he was sure she could feel his.

"There's a lot of mosquitoes out here," he said as they drew apart again.

"I don't mind them so much."

"There might not be so many in the tent."

"Oh."

They went into the tent and sat together on his bed. They kissed again and again, until he moved down her cheek and kissed her on the neck. They reclined together, and he kissed her again on the neck. She murmured in his ear, not words but a sound of happiness. His left hand, which had been resting on her waist, moved up and found her breast. She did not push him away. He held the hand there as they kissed again. Then he moved his hand back down to caress her buttocks, and she pressed against him as they held in a firm, moist kiss.

The fire was casting less light than before, and the tent flap was closed. It was dark in the tent, but they didn't need any light. They fumbled a little, more out of nervousness than lack of light, and they knew what to do in the dark.

Chapter Eight

The man from Wolf River drank his coffee and enjoyed the calm, cool morning. The sun had not yet cleared the cottonwoods east of his camp, and the bluff across the creek had a shadowy, grainy texture that made it look like the cross section of a raw roast of beef. A wisp of smoke rose from the coals of his campfire.

As he drank his coffee, he savored the moments of the night before. It was luscious to remember, but it had all gone so quickly. They had taken off only enough of their clothes to do what they were urgent to do, and when they were done they hadn't waited long to get their clothes in order and come back to sit by the embers. Not long after that, they had gone back to town, walking with the horse following. She had said the mosquitoes were too bad. It had all gone in a flurry, with nervousness and embarrassment afterward. There were good moments to remember, though, including the long kiss when he left her at the hotel. She said she hoped he'd come see her again soon.

He didn't think he needed much persuading. He had enjoyed every way in which he had touched her. He hadn't been with very many women, but he knew that things got better after the first time. One part of him wanted to see

138

her again, and soon.

There was something else in him, though, that nagged. He wondered if he had gone too far. It felt like a continuation of his earlier feeling, when he felt as if he had made sort of a public statement by sticking up for her. Now it was as if he had made a private statement — and in a way, he had — that he would stay with her. He didn't know about that. He knew he wanted to get close to her like that a few more times, but he didn't know if he wanted to be stuck with her, day in and day out, for good.

Life had been easy, just packing up his things when he felt like it and working when and where he liked. It wouldn't be so easy if he had a woman to look out for. He couldn't just drop her when the going got tough, and he didn't want to pick her up if he thought he might get tired of her and want to drop her later on.

Thinking again about how he had felt from the moment he had seen her the day before in the café, he didn't think he would get tired of her that easily. She had grown on him from the first time he had met her. There was a real spark there when he saw her at the kitchen door, and it hadn't gone away when they came out of the tent. He remembered times with other women when it had gone away, when he had wanted to get gone as soon as he had his belt buckled up.

He poured himself another cup of coffee and tried to pick apart what it was that nagged at him. It wasn't just the fear of getting hitched. He thought he knew what that felt like, and it was different. Most men — with the exception of someone like Prunty — wanted to end up with a woman sooner or later, and most of them were probably scared. He had thought about this before, and it seemed like there were two things that scared a man — the idea of not being able to do what he wanted, and the possibility of not making a good choice.

He thought it was the second part that was nagging him now. It was the part that men forgot about when they were head over heels, or the woman was heels in the air. That was how women got men, he knew that. Yet it was something else, and the more he thought about it, the more it seemed like it was a lingering remnant of his original impression that she was low class.

It wasn't just that she was a working girl. He had gone through that idea. If she worked and got dirty, he wasn't that much different. He had grown up knowing that if the dirt came from work, it was nothing to be ashamed of. What was it, then? Was it because she had run off with a man? No, he didn't think so. He probably would have run off with her himself, if he had known her first. But that had something to do with it. Uh-huh. It was like it was in her blood to do something like run off with a man and then fall so easily into the life of a working girl who had no place to go. He wanted to think she had just made a mistake, but he was afraid she might be a little too much like Carter — good looks and good build, but low class in the blood. He wondered if that was the way she looked in the eye of the town, and he thought so. He wondered if it could change — for instance, if they went somewhere else and her circumstances were different — and he thought so. It made him feel bold again.

He smiled and nodded and took another drink of coffee. She was all right. The least he could do was treat her decently and help her get out of this rut. And the best? Well, he could — as the saying went — make an honest woman of her. He wasn't going to decide on that today.

Felver mixed up a batch of biscuits and set the Dutch oven in the coals. They didn't take long to cook, and when they were ready, he ate more than half of them. He didn't have much else to eat at the moment. He realized he had neglected to bring home anything other than his dirty laundry and a girl with her dress pulled up. He laughed at his own joke. She really was a nice girl, more modest than his joke gave her credit for. And anyway, now he had a reason to go to town, and he could drop in to see her while he was at it.

At midmorning, Felver took his horse to water again. He had watered it when he first rolled out of bed, but he thought the horse would appreciate another drink. The sun overhead was warming up the day, and the grass was all dry now in the latter part of July.

As he was putting the horse back out to graze, he saw a rider approaching from the northwest. Given the rider's outline and the direction he was coming from, it looked like Dalhart.

Felver stood by his own horse, his left hand on the picket rope and his right hand on the horse's neck. As the rider came closer, Felver could see it was indeed Dalhart. The horse slowed to a walk at about a quarter mile out, stopped and lifted its tail, and then came in at a slow walk. The men exchanged greetings as the horse came to a stop.

As Dalhart swung off the horse and stepped forward, Felver noticed that his friend had found time to wash his shirt and shave his face. His blue eyes, high cheekbones, and full teeth were all shining, and his chest was swelled out as always, but he had an air of seriousness about him.

"What do you know, Jim?"

"Damn little and not enough."

"Same here. Anything new?"

Dalhart's eyebrows tightened and then relaxed as he said, "A little trouble out at the ranch."

"Really? What kind?"

"Someone robbed the place."

Now it was Felver's eyebrows that went together. "The hell. Did they hold you up?"

"No, they came and smooched some stuff while we were down at the other place, where you were."

"What kind of stuff?" Felver turned and got them walking toward his camp.

"Mostly what they could get their hands on quick-like. Prunty had a little bit of money sacked away, and they got that. Mostly they ransacked the boss's quarters. They took a cash box that had some gold coins, a couple of gold watches, and some cuff links."

Felver nodded. "All the valuables."

"Uh-huh. But on top of that, they took a little picture frame, and that's what's got the boss as mad as anything."

"Was that gold, too?"

"Around the edges, yeah. But it was a picture of the girl he plans to marry."

"Oh, really. I didn't know he had one, but there's no reason he shouldn't."

"Well, he does, and he's mad as hell. He's tryin' to stay levelheaded, though." Dalhart reached into his pocket and brought out his sack of Bull Durham. They had reached the edge of the campsite, so he stopped to roll a cigarette.

"Any idea who it is?"

Dalhart turned down the corners of his mouth and shook his head. "Not yet."

"Has anyone told the sheriff?"

"Oh, yeah. The boss sent me for him right away. I saw your horse in town, but I didn't see

143

you. I peeked into a couple of likely places."

"Must have been while I was soakin' in the tub." Felver laughed. "Less likely place."

Dalhart licked his cigarette and smiled. "I guess so."

"So what did the sheriff say?"

"Oh, nothin' that Clarence couldn't have figured out, except that we wasn't the only place that got hit."

Felver's head went back half an inch, and his eyebrows widened. "Really? Who else got hit?"

Dalhart lit his cigarette and blew away the smoke. "Two other ranches — McCormick and Walker. When everyone at those two places was off at Moran's shindig, these crooks came by and made their move."

"And the sheriff has been out there?"

"Oh, sure. He was the one that told us about it. They took the same kind of stuff at the other places — hard cash, watches, lockets, jewelry, and the like."

Felver nodded. "You figure they hit all three places at about the same time?"

"It makes sense. All the tracks around our place were old. They sacked those other places on the eleventh or twelfth, and that's probably when they hit our place as well."

Felver pursed his lips and then spoke. "Is there any way of knowin' there was more than one of 'em?"

"Nah, but it makes sense. It's a better job for two or three. That way, one of 'em can keep a lookout and hold the horses."

Felver shook his head. "That sounds like something those worthless two, Hodges and Carter, could have done."

"Well, the sheriff looked into them, and they say they were off on a job for Coper, down further south, and he's got a bill of lading to prove it."

"I bet."

"Well, that's the story."

"How about Heid and McNair?"

"The sheriff says Heid was busy at Coper's, helping put on the ice cream social for the visiting minister."

"Uh-huh." McNair seemed more likely anyway, as Felver recalled the comment about taking a crack at the big bastards.

"And there's plenty of people can say McNair didn't leave town the whole time. He doesn't even have a horse."

"That doesn't mean he couldn't ride someone else's." Felver pictured McNair, sitting in the Blue Horse Saloon, and he recalled his impression that the man never left the place. "Well, I guess I could believe he didn't leave town. And as for Heid, it's easy enough to see that he's in the clear, and from what I understand, he doesn't have to lift a finger anyway."

Dalhart nodded. "Isn't that the truth?"

Felver shook his head. "There's got to be other people I don't even know. Did the sheriff look into anyone else?"

"Oh, yeh. There's a couple of other stiffs, but it's the same with them. They stayed in town, and plenty of people saw 'em."

"Well, it's a puzzle, isn't it?"

"Sure is."

"I'd bet Hodges and Carter, but that might be just because I know them." Felver thought for a second, and deciding not to get too stuck on one idea, he thought of another angle. "These other two ranches that got robbed — are they up north, too?"

Dalhart held his cigarette away from his mouth as he nodded. "All three are within ten miles of one another."

"And just about anyone could have known that all three places would be left alone for a couple of days. Well, hell, it could be just about anybody. But it's got me interested."

"That's good."

Felver looked at him. "Why?"

"Because the boss sent me to ask you if you'd like to ride out with me and ask around a little bit."

Felver shrugged. "I'm not doin' much else. Does he actually think he needs me, though?"

"In a way. He says he's got to keep himself out of it, or he might do something he shouldn't."

"Well, I suppose I could."

"He'd put you back on the payroll, of course."

Felver smiled. "That would help. When does my pay start?"

"Today, if you want."

"Well, then I guess I'm back on the job. What do you think we should do first?"

"I think we could go up north, ride around, and ask other people what they might know."

Felver thought of Jenny. He needed to let her know, or she would think he had dropped her. "I guess I could leave my camp here," he said. "I left my other horse in town for safekeeping anyway."

Dalhart nodded as he tossed his cigarette stub in the fire pit and looked around the camp. "I don't think anyone'll bother it."

Felver shrugged. "I don't have anything of value anyway. But I would like to make a little detour into town before we head north."

Dalhart glanced at the sky and then grinned. "It wouldn't hurt to get a bite to eat while we're there."

The two men arrived at the café before the dinner hour, but Nell said she could serve them a full meal. Noticing that Garth, the proprietor, was not at his post, Felver asked if he might step to the kitchen door and speak with Jenny. Nell said to go ahead.

Jenny had an uncertain look on her face as she came to the doorway. She was wearing a white apron over the pale blue dress. As her hands were white with flour, she used the back of her right hand to rub her forehead. "Is there

147

something wrong?" she asked.

"I got called back to work. I don't know for how long."

Her face did not change expression as she said, "Oh."

"I'm leaving my camp where it is, so don't think I'm running off."

Her face relaxed a little. "Well, I wouldn't, if you said you were going to work."

"I just don't know for how long, you see, so I don't want you to worry." Then, realizing he wasn't making anything clearer, he said, "The boss had some things stolen, and he wants someone to ride out with Dalhart and snoop around."

"You won't get hurt, will you?"

"I hope not. I don't think it's somethin' to get shot over, but you don't know."

"Be careful, Owen."

He smiled. "I'll be careful. I want to come back to you in one piece." He held out his hands at waist level, and she put her white, powdery hands in his as their eyes met.

"I trust you," she said.

Her words touched him. "Thanks," he answered. "I feel the same about you."

On his way back to the table, he thought about her words again. They made him feel good, for they told him something about how she felt about herself as well as how she felt about him. As he had interpreted before, she had a sense of dignity; now he understood that she felt that way about herself and about her body. What they had done had meaning; it was worth trust.

After dinner, the two men rode north out of town. With the help of Dalhart's explanations, Felver derived an idea of where the ranches lay with respect to one another. Percy's was the closest to town, northwest about eight miles. Walker's lay almost due north of Percy's another seven miles, while McCormick's was due west of Walker's by six miles. Moran's, where the shindig had taken place, was north of the Walker and McCormick ranches.

Dalhart's idea was to scout around the country between the three ranches that had been robbed. Someone might have seen something.

After they had ridden north for more than an hour, Dalhart pointed to the west and said, "The ranch is off thataway, about two miles. I don't think we need to go there just now."

They rode north another mile, and then Dalhart veered them to the northwest.

"Is McCormick's off this way?" Felver asked.

Dalhart nodded. "Yeah, and I'd like to drop in on some homesteaders that live out this way. I think his name is Gettle."

Felver took in the country around him. It was very much like the country down by his camp and by the claim where they had built the shack. It was rolling plains, with buttes and breaks and some rises big enough to be called

149

hills. It was grassland, with green-leafed trees showing the watercourses. Distant ridges had dark spots suggesting pine and cedar trees, and he had seen a few cedar trees up close on the slopes of dry washes. It was cattle and sheep country — and wild horses, too, he thought, if a fellow got off in the wildest breaks and mesas.

After about half an hour of riding northeast, they topped a rise and stopped.

"Over there," said Dalhart, pointing straight north.

About half a mile away, up against the south side of a tan bluff, sat a house, a shed, and some livestock pens. It looked like a home-steader's place, all right. As they rode closer, Felver noticed more details. The house was no bigger than the shack they had just built for Percy, and the shed in back looked like a com-bination chicken house, shop, and stable. Not a sliver of green grew around the house — no flowers, no trees, no garden. White chickens scratched on the hard ground, and a lone, dirty gray sheep was grazing to the west of the pens.

Dalhart called out as they rode into the yard. A lean man in a flat-crowned, flat-brimmed hat came out from behind the house. He had an ax in his hand, and Felver thought he must have had to go a long ways to find something to use it on, unless he was quartering a beef. On a closer look, he saw that the ax head was clean.

"What can I do for you?" the man called out as the horses came to a stop.

"Name's Dalhart. I met you last year. I ride for George Percy, back over this way. This here's Felver. Your name's Gettle, isn't it?"

The man nodded.

"Mind if we get down?"

"No, go ahead."

The riders dismounted, which was a piece of courtesy that Felver appreciated in Dalhart. There was no call to look down on a man if the conversation was going to last more than a couple of minutes.

"You might have heard," said Dalhart, "that Percy's place and a couple of others got robbed while everyone was gone."

Gettle nodded. "A couple of McCormick's men came by and mentioned it."

Felver thought Gettle was going to say something more, but he didn't. Felver wondered if the homesteader thought he was under suspicion.

"Well," said Dalhart, "they think the same bunch did all three jobs, and they might have been wanderin' around out here along about the eleventh or twelfth."

The man grimaced as he shook his head. "No, they already asked me about it, and I couldn't remember seein' anyone on those two days."

"How about before that?" asked Felver.

"Oh, I don't know. That's been almost two weeks. We see someone come through every few days, it seems like." He twisted his mouth. "Let's go ask."

Gettle turned and walked back toward the house. The two visitors followed him, leading their horses. In back of the house, in the shade of a weathered lean-to, a woman and two blond-headed boys were pulling wool off a dead sheep. The animal had been dead for a day or two, from the smell of it, but its wool was worth something.

"Ruth," the man called.

The woman stood up and came a few steps forward. She was not a bad-looking woman, as Felver saw her, but her dress was dirty and her pale hair was not very well tied behind her head.

"What is it?" she answered.

Her husband looked half at her and half at Dalhart. "How long ago was it that those two young fellas were here? The two that said they were lookin' for stolen cattle?"

The woman glanced at the two visitors. "I don't know."

"Maybe two weeks?"

"Maybe that." The woman stood with her hands in front of her, as if she was trying to cover some of the dirt on her dress.

Gettle turned to look straight at Dalhart. "About two weeks, it sounds like. These two young riders came by, said they were lookin' for stolen cattle. I didn't like their looks, and they didn't look like cowpunchers."

Felver spoke up. "Was one of 'em kind of

heavy, and the other one normal, with high boots?"

The homesteader nodded. "Yeh. That sounds like them."

"Did they say whose cattle they were lookin' for?" asked Dalhart.

"Not that I can remember. They just stood around until I asked them to eat with us, and they did. Not that we had much more than biscuits and beans."

Felver glanced at the wife and the two kids. They looked like a fat-hungry bunch all right, and all three of them gave the newcomers looks of suspicion.

"Did they say anything else?" Dalhart asked.

Gettle shook his head. "No, not really." He glanced at his wife and back. "They just seemed to look too long at things."

Dalhart's face had a half-smile as he looked at Felver. "Sounds like Poodgie and Pookie, doesn't it?"

Felver grimaced. "It does."

The other man did not show any humor. "They didn't give any names that I remember. I was just glad to see 'em go."

"I don't blame you," said Dalhart, "if it's the ones we're thinkin' of. They've got other names, of course."

"I imagine."

Back on the trail, when they were well enough away from the homestead, Felver said, "That was a sad little outfit, wasn't it?"

"I'd say. But there's worse."

"I sort of feel sorry for 'em. That dead sheep is probably a big loss for them."

"Probably so," Dalhart agreed. "But that's the trouble with them sheep. They just love to die."

Felver remembered the hide they had dug up back at the work camp, and he wondered what Gettle had been using the ax for. "It doesn't look as if these people have had the good fortune to butcher anyone else's beef lately."

Dalhart sniffed. "Probably not since winter. They're probably pretty careful."

"What do you think about that hide we dug up the other day?"

"Oh, it was probably someone like this, but just not as cautious."

Felver recalled Percy's attitude. "It's hard to think of it as a real theft, isn't it?"

"Oh, yeah. It's not that much of a crime. Not like these sonsofbitches we're lookin' for now."

"You mean Poodgie and Pookie?"

"A man shouldn't say anything before he's sure, and that's why I didn't want to mention any names back there. And it's probably not fair to say right now that I think so-'n'-so done it, if they have an alibi for the eleventh and twelfth."

"But it seems like they were out in the neighborhood, lookin' things over, not too long before that."

"It sure does."

As they rode on, Felver thought again about the homesteader family he had seen. They were stuck in his mind, those people who had their sense of pride even if they were poor. Maybe they were the kind who would be poor no matter what, but they worked for what they had. There were others like them, scattered across the country, trying to scratch out a living. It didn't seem right, he thought, that there were poor folks in the world who worked like hell and stayed half hungry, while there were others who would steal more than they needed and probably sell it for less than its value.

Dalhart was right about not jumping to conclusions or naming names too soon. Call them Poodgie and Pookie for the time being, and try to get to the bottom of it. A man couldn't fix all the wrongs in the world, but he might be able to help run this one down.

Chapter Nine

Felver and Dalhart rode on a few more miles until they came to a small creek, where they stopped to water the horses and take a rest. Dalhart rolled and lit a cigarette, then found a dry stick of sagebrush and squatted in the shade of his horse.

"Let's figger it out," he said, brushing the stick back and forth on the ground to clear a spot to scratch on.

Felver, squatting in the shade of his own horse, said, "I've counted back, and I'm pretty sure they delivered the window on the eleventh."

"That sounds right. We started that work on the tenth, and they showed up the second day."

"Once they made sure of where we were, they could have come up here on the twelfth and done all three in a day. In fact, I'd think they'd want to do it all in one day."

Dalhart was scratching at the ground as if it were a map and a calendar both. "That sounds right. Now, how about earlier, when they were up at Gettle's?"

"The homesteader's? He said it was two weeks ago, which would be the fifth. Give or take a day, and they probably wouldn't have been there on the Fourth of July."

156

"Uh-huh." Dalhart took a thoughtful drag on his cigarette.

"So put it on the fifth or sixth. I came to town on the sixth, and I didn't see them until the second day, which was the seventh."

"What about Coper?" Dalhart jabbed in the middle of his sketching.

"I'd bet his bill of lading says the twelfth." Felver looked at Dalhart's scratchings as if the answer were hidden in there somewhere. "You know, I keep coming back to this feeling that Coper's got something to do with it, but I can't figure the connection. I can't imagine why he'd hire them in the first place, and if he's givin' 'em an alibi, I can't understand why. And if they've got an alibi, we can't very well go up to them and say, 'Look here, we think you did this thing, and we need to ask you some questions.' But we're goin' to have to do somethin' like that."

Dalhart smoked on his cigarette and nodded. "That's pretty much how I see it."

Felver shook his head. "So it looks like we're goin' to have to find someone with the goods on him, if we're goin' to get to the bottom of this. We can ask questions, but I don't know how far it'll get us."

When Dalhart finished his cigarette, they mounted up and rode on. Always as they rode, Felver searched the terrain, as if they were looking for lost cattle or horses. At the same time, he knew the answer was not there. The perpetrators had ridden across some stretch of this country a week or so earlier, but they hadn't left any visible proof. Felver looked at the ground and saw the shadows that he and Dalhart and their horses were casting. That was how fleeting the evidence was, he thought — like a shadow on the grass.

As they rode on, Felver tried to picture the type of person or persons who would do this kind of job. A fellow had to have just about no regard for someone else's privacy to be able to go into a person's living quarters, toss through his belongings, and make off with items of personal value like watches, lockets, and pictures. It was easy to imagine Hodges and Carter at that sort of work. They had had no shame at all in saying they had followed the girl because she was supposed to give them something — and then there was the remark about Felver being a whoremonger. Whether the girl had ever had relations with him or any other man was her business, not theirs, but they showed no respect for personal boundaries.

Felver found himself wanting to fight again, and he had to tell himself to try to keep a clear view of things. As he and Dalhart had both said in separate ways, he couldn't just come out and say he thought so-and-so was a thief, and he had to be careful not to let his own feelings cloud his view. Then he would have a problem with his own pot a-boilin' too easily.

Dalhart took them across country now, to the

northwest, to another homestead. From there they went west to another, and then south to another. In all three places, the answer was the same: there might have been someone out here a couple of weeks earlier, but there hadn't been anyone conspicuous on the eleventh or the twelfth.

The sun was almost touching the horizon as the two riders headed south from the last homestead. The grassland lay calm and still on all sides, and the only sounds were the clop of horse hooves and the squeak of saddle leather.

"I don't know what we thought we were going to find," said Felver, "but I guess we did better than nothing."

"I imagine. At least we've got somethin' to tell the boss."

"Is the ranch house pretty much south of us by now?"

Dalhart yawned and nodded. "About five miles."

They rode on as the sun went down. Dalhart's horse picked up a good pace, and Felver's horse joined in. Shadows had disappeared and dusk was thickening as the men rode into the ranch yard. They put their horses away and went to the ranch house, where lamps were already lit for the evening, and the smell of food was on the air.

Clarence looked up from the supper table, where he had already sat down to join the boss and Prunty. "Hurry up, boys. It's goin' fast."

Felver glanced at the platter and saw a heap of fried meat. He connected what he saw with what he smelled. "Liver?" he asked as he sat down.

"That's right," said Clarence. "Bill killed a beef today, and we always eat the liver first." He looked at Felver as if there might be some objection.

"Good," Felver said, spearing a crusted slice for himself.

Clarence looked at Dalhart and said, "You don't look like you did any damn good."

Dalhart shook his head. "Not much." Then he looked at Percy and said, "We covered quite a bit of country. Stopped in at four places. No one had anything to say except Gettle. He said there was a couple riders out this way right after the fourth, but he didn't see anything on the eleventh or twelfth."

"Oh," said Percy, barely looking up. "Any idea who they were, or what they were up to?"

Dalhart took a small piece of liver to go with his large serving of potatoes. "Gettle said they were out lookin' for stolen cattle. From the description, it sounds like the two boys that delivered a window."

Clarence's mouth hung open, showing his yellow teeth. "Them little bastards," he said.

"Not to mention names," Dalhart went on, "but Felver and I counted back, and they delivered it on the eleventh."

Percy looked up and nodded. "They did."

Dalhart cut off a small piece of liver and paused before putting it into his mouth. "We're sure they've got an alibi, but we think it's worth followin' up on."

Percy's eyes looked troubled, but his voice was calm. "Like you say, you don't want to jump to conclusions, but it's worth looking into."

Dalhart chewed and swallowed. "Probably the best time to go into town is the afternoon, so if you've got somethin' you want done in the mornin', that could fit in."

Percy glanced across the table. "Bill was going to go check on a water hole over west. You don't need any help, do you, Bill?"

Felver looked at Prunty, whom he had hardly ever seen without a hat. The man's high, pale forehead was noticeable in contrast with the weathered face and pointed chin.

"No, not at all," said Prunty in his strained voice.

The boss looked back at Dalhart. "Well, if it's just for half a day, I could send the two of you back out north to check cattle. You could be back here for dinner and then go into town after that."

Felver slept in the bunkhouse that night, amid Clarence's snoring and Prunty's wheezed nasal breathing. He heard Clarence get up in the middle of the night, but otherwise the ranch house was still and quiet.

In the morning after breakfast, Felver saddled a pale, cream-colored horse and rode out with Dalhart, who had picked out a bay. They rode north and a little east, where the grass was good. Nothing looked out of order, and they saw no other riders from the time they left the ranch till the time they got back.

At dinner, Percy looked at Dalhart and said, "Clarence wants to ride in with you two boys. He wants to pick up a few things."

Dalhart glanced at the cook and then at the boss. "Do we need to take the wagon?"

"I don't think so. You said you would just ride in, didn't you, Clarence?"

The older man looked as if he was practicing good behavior. He even had his hair combed down, although it didn't look as if he had washed it since coming back from the work camp. "Sure," he said. "It won't be any trouble."

After dinner, Prunty roped out and saddled a little brown horse for Clarence. Dalhart picked out a fresh horse for himself, while Felver saddled his own horse, which had had a chance to rest up.

Once he had fought his way into the saddle, Clarence looked like a natural rider. His horse gave him no trouble, and he said very little on his way into town. As they rode into the main street, Dalhart asked him what he needed to buy, and he said there was no hurry.

Felver said the Doubloon was the only place he had seen a certain pair, so the three riders tied up their horses outside the saloon and walked in. There were no other patrons in the place.

Dalhart looked at Felver and asked, "Shall we stay?"

Felver, who didn't think it was a good idea to show right away that they were looking for someone, nodded and said, "I think so."

The three men stood at the bar, with Clarence in the middle and Dalhart closest to the door. Felver asked for a beer, and the other two ordered whiskey. They stood in silence as the bartender fetched their drinks. Felver looked up and saw the painting of the pirate and his telescope, as did the other two men, but no one said anything about it.

After a short while in the Doubloon, the three men finished their drinks and walked out into the afternoon glare. They stayed on the board sidewalk and walked past the café, where Felver paused to look in through the window. He saw no one but the waitress, who was bending her ample body over a table as she wiped it.

Next they went to the doorway of the Blue Horse Saloon, where they paused before going into the shadowy world inside. Four men were strung along the bar, and no one sat at the tables. Felver did not know any of the men, so he turned and asked Dalhart, "Shall we have another?"

Dalhart said yes, and Clarence, still the

model of good behavior, said nothing. The men went inside, ordered their drinks, and leaned on the bar.

About fifteen minutes later, a silhouette in a billed cap appeared at the doorway. Felver recognized the person as McNair, and as the man walked in, Felver realized it was the first time he had seen McNair up and away from the table. McNair had a noticeable movement, as he was an inch or two shorter than average and walked with his arms out at his side and his legs springing at the knees. He looked up and down the bar and then at each man as he bounced by. When he came to Felver he gave a half-smile and nodded, then went on to take a seat at a table away from the bar and facing the door.

Felver turned to Dalhart, who stood at his right. He said, "His pal ought to be along in a while. If we don't get anyone else to talk to, those two might be worth a few minutes of our time."

Dalhart looked straight ahead at the mirror and nodded.

Felver followed Dalhart's glance to the mirror. He could see Clarence, on the other side of Dalhart, staring at his drink as he rested his forearms on the bar. Felver remembered one saloon he had been in that had stools along the bar, and he thought more places should have seats like that for stove-up old fellows who might drink themselves woozy.

They finished their drinks and ordered another round. Not long after that, a figure in a bowler hat appeared at the door, and Felver recognized Heid. The young man walked in with something of a light step, as if he had just sent a dozen roses to a banker's daughter. With his watch chain, vest, and hat, he looked almost dapper, a bit of dust and dirt notwithstanding. He nodded to each man at the bar as he walked by, and he gave a twitch of his mustache as he passed Felver, who nodded back.

Felver watched in the mirror as Heid took a seat at McNair's table. Before long, the bartender took an empty glass and a full bottle to the table. Having seen the routine twice now, Felver imagined that Heid bought the larger share of the drinks — or, as he thought of it a second way, both of them drank off of Coper.

Felver turned to Dalhart. "Do you get along with those two well enough to go sit at their table?"

Dalhart stretched his face down and nodded.

"Well, let's give it a try."

Dalhart turned and said something to Clarence, who said something in a low voice. Dalhart turned back to Felver and said, "Clarence says he'll wait here at the bar."

Felver, remembering McNair's comments about Clarence, and imagining that the disdain might be mutual, said in a low voice, "It's probably just as well."

As they approached the table, Heid looked

165

up and waved them on. After an exchange of greetings, Felver and Dalhart sat down.

"Looks like you lads have a day off," said Heid. Then, turning directly to Felver, he said, "I take it you're still working for Percy."

"Right on both counts," said Felver. "I'm workin' but I'm not."

"Best part of any job," said McNair, who had just rolled a smoke and now lit a match.

Heid turned to Dalhart. "And what's new in the world of cattle and horses?"

"Not much," said Dalhart, taking out his own bag of tobacco. "At least, in that area."

"Oh?" said Heid, leaning back and reaching into his vest pocket.

Felver thought he was going to bring out his pipe, which he had a tendency to do at dramatic moments. Instead, he took out his watch, held it at the length of its chain, and wound it.

Dalhart shook grains of tobacco into his troughed cigarette paper. "Yeh. You probably heard there was some personal items stolen at some of the ranches up north."

Heid pushed out his mustache as he finished winding the watch. "Yes, I did hear something about that. Did Percy lose some valuables, too?"

"Yep. Him and Prunty both, for that matter."

McNair spoke up. "Well, where is he today? Now that I think of it, I didn't see his smilin' face as I came in."

"I reckon he's back at the ranch." Dalhart

looked back at Heid. "Anyway, that's what's new," he said, and he went back to work on his cigarette.

Now the pipe came out. "Well, that's too bad."

Dalhart looked up from his work and gave a stern look. "I just wish to hell I knew who it was."

Heid blew air through his empty pipe. "I hope you don't think I had anything to do with it."

"Oh, no," said Dalhart, smoothing down the seam he had just licked. "I wouldn't have said that if I did."

"As I recall," said Heid, "that happened while the visiting minister was in town."

"I remember," said McNair. "You were so busy with the Lord's work that I had to sit in here by myself."

Felver looked at the two of them. It was already well known that they all had their alibis. Coper had everyone covered but McNair, and he had been in plain view. It was funny, he thought, that every time something smelled fishy, Coper seemed to lurk somewhere in the background. Thinking he might catch someone off guard, Felver asked, "Have you seen Coper lately?"

Heid rapped his pipe upside down in his palm. "No. Why do you ask?"

"I thought you might have asked him about hauling your equipment."

Heid sniffed as he wiped his hand on his trouser leg. "No, not really. I didn't really have that in mind. But to answer your question more fully, he went to Denver. The minister was going back, so Coper took the opportunity to give him some company."

"Took the opportunity," said Dalhart, lighting a match.

"I believe he goes to Denver from time to time anyway, on business. At any rate, I expect him to be back in the next few days. He's usually gone a week to ten days."

"That's the way it is when a man's got business," said Dalhart.

"Or when he wants to get away," sniped McNair. "Out of the public eye."

Heid had brought out his tobacco pouch and was now dipping into it with the bowl of his pipe. "Sort of like the polar bear when he's frolickin' on the equator."

"Meanin'?" said Dalhart.

"He gets a long ways from home, he gets a tent in his pants," said McNair.

Felver doubted that Coper needed a warmer or distant climate to bring on that effect, but he said nothing.

Dalhart laughed. "Then I don't suppose he'd want to spare the horses until he got rid of the preacher."

Heid's eyebrows flickered. "That one, anyway."

"Well, I hope he enjoys his trip," said Felver.

"He could stay gone," said McNair, "and no-body would miss him. That's the way with any of these mucky-mucks. No one needs 'em. Everyone else does the work. They think the world would fall apart without 'em, but it doesn't."

"There's an old story about that," said Heid, pointing the stem of his pipe at McNair. "This is a good story for you." He looked at the other two as he held his unlit, loaded pipe in his right hand. "There was an emperor of one of those old empires — China, I think — who died. No one knew it except his prime minister, who hid the body away in a cave and didn't tell anyone. Then for a whole year he gave all the orders, and the country ran along smooth, and no one knew any better. After a year, he takes out the old king's skeleton, and he says, 'Look here. This country's been run by a dead man for a whole year. It's really been me that's been running things, so don't you think you ought to make me the emperor?' The people said sure, and as soon as they got him into his crown and his robe and all, they killed him." Heid paused and lit his pipe. Then through the cloud of smoke he said, "They could see how good it was to have things run by a dead man, and they wanted things to stay that good."

McNair's sunken eyes had lit up. "That's a hell of a good story."

"I didn't come up with it myself," said Heid, almost apologetically. "I just heard it some-

169

where, and I thought I'd pass it along."

McNair's fire was going now. "Well, it's a damn good story and a true one, wherever it came from. It tells you how much you really need those drones at the top. It could fit a lot of people."

Felver looked at Heid and McNair and decided to try something. "It reminds me of a joke," he said, "but I can't remember the whole thing. It goes something like this. The father is always taking the servant girl into the pantry, and the son is always eavesdropping. Then the father dies, and the kid doesn't tell anyone right away, so he can sneak into the pantry that night and take the father's place. He figures once he's had the girl, he can light a candle and show her who he really is. But he's not in there but a few minutes, and she says 'Why aren't you doing it as well as you usually do? Is it because your son isn't out there listening?' "

Dalhart gave a short laugh that might have been either nervous or uncertain, and the other two barely laughed enough to be polite.

"Well, I thought it was funnier," said Felver. "Maybe I didn't tell it right."

"Oh, it's funny," said McNair. "But more likely it was the kid who was always gettin' the servant girl, and the old man got so excited it gave him a fit and carried him off."

"Well, I could probably think about it and rework it," said Felver.

"Yeah," said McNair. "I think when a man

gets old enough to have a kid who can do that kind of work, he's probably all fagged out and doesn't have any beans left."

Felver thought he was getting closer to some of the attitudes he wanted to uncover. He was sure there was more resentment of Coper than had come to light yet, and he thought he might be on his way to knowing more. "How old does a man get," he asked, "when he doesn't have any beans anymore?"

Heid must have been waiting for him. He palmed the bowl of his pipe and puffed out a cloud. "Oh, about like your friend Clarence."

Felver made a quarter-turn, out of reflex, to glance at Clarence, but the old man was gone.

"Damn," said Dalhart, who had also turned. "I wonder where he went."

Felver and Dalhart looked at each other. "I could give you one guess," said Felver. Both men stood up and tossed off their drinks. Felver glanced at the other two men still seated. "Gentlemen, it's been a pleasure, but I think we'd better go look for that old man before he gets into trouble."

McNair smirked and said, "See you later."

Heid gave his exaggerated somber nod and said, "Always a pleasure."

As Felver and Dalhart clomped along the sidewalk toward the Doubloon, Dalhart said, "I thought he was actin' too nice. He just can't stay out of it, that's what."

"And he's probably had enough to drink to

171

get himself pretty well primed."

"Thank God he's not wearing a gun," said Dalhart, who had originally suggested they all leave their guns in their saddlebags.

When they arrived at the doorway of the Doubloon, Felver saw Clarence right away. He was standing behind two men who were leaning on the bar with their backs to him. Felver recognized the two men as Hodges and Carter. They were the middle two of six or seven men standing along the bar.

Clarence, with a glass of whiskey in his hand, was standing in a slouch. As Felver and Dalhart walked up to him, he made a show of ignoring them.

"I'm talking to you," he said.

Hodges and Carter showed no reaction, and with no mirror behind the bar, Felver could not tell whether they knew who else had arrived.

"Come on, Clarence," said Dalhart.

"I'm not done," said the older man. "I've got somethin' to say to these whelps."

"I don't think you need to say anything," Felver said. "Why don't you just give me your drink, and we'll get out of here."

Clarence turned a wide eye on Felver. "And why don't you just go to hell? I paid for this drink, and I'm goin' to drink it." He lifted his chin toward the bar. "And besides, I'm not done with these two."

"You ought to be," said Dalhart.

"By God, Jim, you're not gonna tell me what

to do, or I'll whip your ass, too."

Dalhart raised his eyebrows and said nothing.

"Come on, Clarence," Felver said. "Let's go."

Clarence took an unsteady drink. "Not yet. I've got to finish with these two snivelers."

Hodges turned around. "Look, old man. Why don't you leave with your two nursemaids, and go home and piss in your beard?"

Clarence stood for a second with his mouth open, and then he said, "I'm not afraid of you tinhorns."

Carter turned around. "You ought to be. The more you open your mouth, the more likely you are to get hurt."

"Look," said Felver, "we're trying to get him out of here."

Carter turned his tight plum face at Felver. "Why don't you, then? Why don't the three of you hop on your horses and get the hell out of town?"

Felver didn't have an answer right away.

Clarence said, "I'll leave. In just a minute. Soon as I say what I want to say."

Felver put his hand on Clarence's sleeve. "Come on, now. You've said enough already."

Clarence tucked his arm away from Felver's reach. "Careful, boy. You leave your hands off me."

Felver lowered his hands to his side. He felt like clobbering the old man and dragging him out of the bar, but then he felt guilty at the idea of roughing up an old drunk man. He looked at Dalhart and imagined the Texan felt the same.

"Now," said Clarence, with his drink still in his hand. "Who's gonna piss in whose beard?"

Hodges, still with his back to the bar, shifted his weight and started to talk. "If you —"

His words were cut off when Clarence flung a spray of whiskey in his face.

Before Felver could do a thing, Hodges had moved forward and slapped the glass out of Clarence's hand. The glass flew ten feet away and crashed on the floor. Then, with his left hand, Hodges slapped Clarence on the side of his head. Hodges had moved quickly and then stopped.

Tension hung in the air for a moment. No need to make it worse, thought Felver, if they could get Clarence out at this point.

Clarence had rocked back on his heels and now stood, weaving, with his mouth open. "You don't scare me," he said, "you common little —"

Hodges moved forward, again with surprising quickness, and with both hands gave Clarence a powerful shove. The old man staggered back, fell against a table and chairs, and then slumped to the floor.

Felver and Dalhart had moved between Clarence and the two men at the bar. Dalhart leaned to pick up the old man, while Felver faced the other two.

"I think that's enough," he said. "I hope you're proud of yourself, slapping around an old drunk man."

Hodges turned his droopy eyes on Felver. "He's just lucky he didn't say any more."

Felver looked at Clarence, whose hat was down over his eyes. "Maybe we're all lucky," he said.

With a little less starch in him now, Clarence let Felver and Dalhart haul him out of the saloon and put him on his horse. The sun was still up and bright, just about to slip in the western sky.

When they were safely out of town, Felver shook his head and said to Dalhart, "Well, that botched everything up. We didn't get to finish with Heid and McNair, and we didn't even get started with those other two."

Dalhart rubbed his jaw. "It could have been worse, I guess." After a moment he spoke again. "By the way, where did you hear that joke about the girl in the pantry?"

"Oh, I didn't hear that anywhere. I made it up. That's why it wasn't very funny."

Chapter Ten

Felver thought the boss showed good composure when he found out what happened. He nodded, looked at Clarence, and said, "There's not much we can do about it now. It looks like you ought to go rest for a while, Clarence, and sleep it off."

Clarence went to his bunk, and Prunty rustled up the grub for supper. It consisted of cold leftover liver, cold biscuits, and some warmed-up beans that smelled as if they'd been kept around at least one day too long.

When the four men sat down to eat, Percy said, "I wish Clarence hadn't done that. You boys may or may not turn something up, but it sounds as if he set back your chances. Each day that goes by whittles down the chances that we'll be able to recover anything."

The boss stuck a chunk of cold fried liver in the middle of his warm beans, cut the liver into small pieces, and mixed up the mess. Before he took a bite he said, "I'd like you boys to go back out tomorrow and see what you can get out of those two. I'll send Bill with you, to keep the odds in our favor. Take your guns but don't wear them."

Felver looked at Dalhart, who had served himself only biscuits and beans. Dalhart gave a little shrug and nodded. Felver then looked at Prunty, who was cutting up liver into his beans just as the boss had done. It didn't look like very much fun scheduled for the next day, but Prunty wouldn't be the sort of handicap that Clarence had been. If anything, he would reduce the amount of nonsense just with his joyless presence.

Felver went to bed with the taste of liver in his mouth. He didn't dislike liver as Dalhart did, but it wasn't his favorite meat. Supper had been one of those meals that was just taking up space. That was all right, but to keep things in balance, a fellow needed a really satisfying meal once in a while. Felver thought back to the steak and gravy he had fixed when Jenny came to breakfast. Now, that was good, he thought. Maybe there were more things in it that the body craved.

Some things were like that. He remembered a time when he was with the Mexicans, down in New Mexico. They had had a big fiesta for their independence day, September 16, and he had stayed up all night drinking and dancing with them. Then he had slept a few hours and had dragged himself to the table. A wrinkled, smiling señora had dished him up some pork meat and chile verde from one clay pot and some frijoles from another. It was one of the most memorable meals he had ever eaten. It satisfied everything his body seemed to be craving after a night of drinking, dancing, and little sleep. After the señora served him up twice, he went outside and sat in the shade and thought he could live like that for a long time if he had to. As it turned out, he didn't have to. The Mexicans went back to work, the girl he thought he was in love with turned out to be married, and Felver thought he had better get back to the Wolf River country before the cold weather set in.

Felver had remembered that meal many times since then. Usually he remembered it at times like this, when the taste of a poor meal hung around in his mouth. He thought that if he had to eat Prunty's fixin's for very long, he could easily run away with the Mexicans and learn their ways.

Then he thought of Jenny and smiled. There was no need to run off with the Mexicans if she was around. Between the two of them, they could fix up some pretty good grub. She said she hadn't done much cooking, but he imagined she was learning now. And he could turn out a decent meal himself. He thought again of the steaks and gravy. That had been a damn good meal, one of the best he had had this year, he thought. Come to think of it, it had a little pork fat in it. So did the Mexican food. And both of them had gravy and sauce. Maybe that was it — keep things just a little greasy and a little moist. He laughed to himself. Those were things to be thinking about in a place like this.

In the morning, Clarence was back in the

kitchen, surly as ever. He criticized the whole crew for not eating fresh meat the night before. They had a whole animal hanging, he said, and some of it was bound to spoil. He fried up a huge stack of steaks and a mound of sliced potatoes. Then he set out two plates of biscuits, and not long after that he brought out a pan of gravy. Felver thought it was Clarence's way of doing penance, at least for not having fixed supper the night before. It was a hearty meal, and everybody dug in, including Prunty.

After breakfast, the three hired hands went to saddle their horses. Felver decided to ride his own horse again, as it hadn't worked much the day before. He checked his six-shooter and gunbelt, which he had left in his saddlebag. Dalhart checked his also, and Prunty put his in its place.

"I don't know," said Felver. "If we'd been wearing guns yesterday, somebody might've gotten shot. But if we go back lookin' for those two today, they might think we're lookin' for trouble, and they've always got a gun on their hip."

"They could get trigger happy," said Dalhart. "But I think the boss's idea all along has been to have someone else go along, not so much to even the fight as to give the other party the idea that there's witnesses. I don't think they'll shoot someone that's unarmed, not in plain view, anyway — and especially if we catch 'em early in the day, before they've had much to drink."

Felver nodded and then looked at Prunty, who was putting the bit into his horse's mouth. He had no idea how well Prunty could use his fists or his gun either one, but he thought it was a good backup to have a third man, especially someone as hard to bend as Prunty.

The three of them rode out of the ranch while the morning was young. Felver had to tip his hat forward to get shade for his eyes. Dalhart, who had fallen in on Felver's left, had his hat tipped forward also. Felver looked back at Prunty, who rode behind them. Prunty's hat brim was permanently turned down in front, and he rode with a bit of a slouch, so not much of his face was visible.

Dalhart spoke over his shoulder. "You know, Bill, the boss wants us to make sure we all get to the whorehouse today."

Prunty mumbled something but did not raise his head.

They rode on without speaking. The sound of horse hooves lifted on the morning air. Occasionally a horse shook his bridle or snorted, but there was no other sound until Dalhart spoke again.

"I don't know if they stay in town or what they do. I suppose one of us could ask around."

Felver glanced at Prunty and then at Dalhart. "I'm sure you know more people than the rest of us do."

When they rode into town, the main street showed a little life. Men were sweeping the sidewalk in front of a couple of businesses, and two wagons were parked in the middle of the street in front of Five Star Drayage. Felver wondered if Coper was back from Denver, but he saw nothing but dark windows beneath the wood overhang. Down the street, the door of the Doubloon lay open upon a dark interior.

Dalhart led the riders to that spot, and swinging down, he said, "It looks like someone's cleanin' out the place, so I'll just pop in there and ask 'em."

He wasn't gone long. In a few minutes he came back out into the sunlight, pulled his hat forward, and stepped into the street. As Felver handed him the reins he said, "They've got a camp out here south of town." Dalhart swung into the saddle and adjusted his reins. He looked back at Prunty, who gave a faint nod but said nothing.

They rode out of town to the south, crossing the creek and following a wagon road. A little ways out, Dalhart said, "I'd just as soon have a smoke before we get there. How 'bout you, Bill?"

"Suits me," said Prunty.

The sun was climbing now, and Felver could feel sweat trickling down his back. He swung down from the saddle and moved his horse around, then squatted in the shade. Dalhart did likewise, then dug into his pocket and brought out his makin's. Felver looked at Prunty, who

181

stood off by himself in the sun with his head lowered as he rolled a cigarette.

"Can't help feelin' a little nervous," Dalhart said. "What with us goin' lookin' for 'em."

Felver glanced at Prunty. "They might think we're comin' back to even the score, but they'll find out soon enough we're not lookin' for a fight." He spoke loud enough for Prunty to hear so that the lean rider wouldn't think the other two were speaking just between them. "If you want, I'll talk to 'em."

"All right with me," said Dalhart.

Felver looked at Prunty, who raised his head this time and nodded.

When Dalhart and Prunty had finished their smoke, the three men mounted up and continued south. About two miles out of town, Dalhart pointed to the right and said, "See those trees? There's a little dribble of a crick over there, and that's where they're supposed to have their camp."

Felver nodded and turned halfway in his saddle. "Let's spread out just a little."

They rode toward the trees, and at about fifty yards away, Felver called out. Seeing two horses tied to trees, he imagined someone was there. He stopped his horse to wait for an answer, as did Dalhart and Prunty.

The call came back, so Felver and the other two rode closer. The camp came into view now. It was a dirty camp, with tin cans and whiskey bottles in a heap. The horses stood off to the right of camp, while the trash heaps sat on the left. Beyond the trash heap, Felver saw scraps of paper and dark little piles. Little pigs, he thought. They didn't even bury their waste.

Hodges and Carter were standing on either side of the fire pit — Carter on the right and Hodges on the left. They were wearing their guns as always, and they were looking over the visitors, no doubt checking to see if anyone was armed.

Closer now, Felver saw that the cans and bottles had been shot up. A stack of firewood lay beyond the fire pit, and all of it was jagged and broken. Something behind Carter caught Felver's eye. He saw that it was a deer carcass hanging from a tree, turning black. The backstraps had been cut out, and now flies were hovering around the carcass and landing on it.

"What do you want?" came the challenge from Carter.

"A few words," said Felver, dismounting.

Hodges shifted his weight and said, "If you came out on account of the old man, you can forget it. He had it coming, and worse."

Dalhart and Prunty dismounted and stood about five yards away on either side of Felver.

"That's not why we came," Felver answered.

"Well, what is it, then?" asked Carter, in his taunting tone.

Felver turned, and as he did so he remembered the two men's method of working back and forth. "We've got a few questions."

"Talk's cheap," said Hodges.

Felver looked at him and said, "For you, maybe." Then he looked at Carter's tight face and pig eyes. "Now, I'll tell you what's on our mind. As you no doubt know, our boss and a few others had some personal items stolen a while back, and we're hopin' to find out a few things."

Carter smirked. "Well you're just a regular little detective, aren't you?" He spit to the side. "You think we haven't been questioned already? Hell, the sheriff picked on us right away, and he knows he was wastin' his time. They say those places got hit on the eleventh or twelfth, and we were workin' both those days."

"And we've already proved it," said Hodges. "It's none of your business to begin with, and even less so now."

"Maybe," said Felver. He turned back to Carter, still with the idea of trying to keep the lead rather than let them pull him back and forth. He focused again on the pig eyes as he spoke. "Nobody's accusing anybody, but we've got a right to ask a few questions on behalf of our boss."

"Well, you've asked 'em," said Carter.

"Not all of them." Felver thought he saw a little flinch, so he waited a second to let the comment sink in. Then he said, "We're wondering what you were doing up in that country the week before, say along about the fifth or sixth."

184

Hodges's voice came blurting. "Who says we were there?"

Felver flicked him a glance. "Doesn't matter." Bearing down again on Carter, he said, "What were you doing there?"

"It's none of your business. Maybe we were just out for a ride."

"Were you working for any of the ranches out there?"

"Go to hell," snapped Hodges.

Felver ignored him. "Well, were you?" he asked Carter. "You know we've asked around, so tell me."

Carter glanced at the other two riders and back at Felver. "Hell, no. Of course we weren't working for any ranches."

"Then why did you say you were looking for stolen cattle? Whose cattle would you be looking for?"

Carter's face turned dark and started looking like a plum again. "It's none of your damn business where we went or what we said to anyone. And furthermore, I've never touched anything of yours, or anything you even thought was yours."

Felver's face tensed at the allusion. He could feel the anger now, starting to build up inside. This was the moment at which he always wanted to fight. Carter was good at it.

"I lost something." It was Prunty's voice, dry and strained.

Carter turned his tight face at Prunty. "Are

you sayin' I took it?"

"I'm sayin' someone did."

Carter pointed at him. "Well, you'd better be careful with what you say, or you'll have to back it up."

Prunty nodded. "I'm not an old drunk."

Carter raised his fists. He wasn't wearing his wrist cuffs at the moment. "Well, come on, then, mush-mouth," he said.

Felver had a sense that Carter was in for a surprise. Prunty hardly ever spoke that much, so he must have had a lot building up inside, not to mention whatever ill temper he carried around with him by nature.

Prunty stepped forward with a wide-swinging blow that landed square on Carter's cheekbone. The hat went flying, and Carter staggered back two steps. His eyes narrowed as he stepped forward, bringing up his fists again. Prunty came back with the same right punch, thudding his fist on the side of Carter's head like a hammer blow. This time Carter went back and down. He got up onto his left elbow and reached for his gun.

"I wouldn't do it," called Dalhart.

Felver looked around, and he saw Dalhart standing with his horse as a shield and with his six-gun leveled across the saddle.

"You either," he said, swinging the barrel toward Hodges. "Now, if you boys want to have a fair fight, have it."

Nobody moved.

Dalhart spoke again. "Take off your gunbelts, and I'll put this thing away. Then we'll see if anybody wants some more."

"I'll fight that skinny bastard," said Hodges. He unbuckled his gunbelt, pulled the thong that held his holster to his leg, and set the belt and holster on the ground. Then he set his hat on top of his gun. His droopy eyes looked dull, and his fat lips tucked back at the corners in a sneer.

Prunty took off his hat and vest without a word.

"Just a minute," said Dalhart. "We've got another piece we got to set aside."

Everyone looked at Carter, who was sitting up now. He took off his gunbelt and set it on the ground.

"Good enough," said Dalhart, and his pistol dropped out of sight.

Hodges had his fists up now. "C'mon, c'mon," he said, opening his right fist and beckoning with his fingers.

Prunty did just that, swinging a blow at Hodges's head. Hodges raised his left arm and leaned to the right, so Prunty's fist thudded on his shoulder. Prunty stepped back and came at it again, as if it were the only punch he knew how to throw. Again Hodges evaded the worst of it, but Prunty surprised him then with a left hook.

As Hodges straightened up, his guard came down. Prunty hit him again with the heavy right hammer, and this time he landed it on Hodges's jaw. The heavy man stepped back and raised his fists high. Prunty took the opportunity to drive his left fist into Hodges's belly.

Both men stepped back, and it looked as if Hodges was still in the fight. He was breathing hard, but the big punch to the head hadn't dazed him.

"C'mon," he said again.

Prunty came back one more time with the swinging right. Hodges leaned away from it, and as he did so he managed to shoot out a left jab that caught Prunty full in the mouth as he was lunging forward. Prunty stepped back.

Hodges got set and led with his left. He held his right arm a little lower, cocked and making small, circular motions.

Prunty did not close in now. It looked as if he was throwing his punch short until it cracked on Hodges's forearm. Hodges winced and brought the arm back up. Prunty hit it again and again. He stepped back and came back in with a swinging left punch. It caught Hodges on the side of his face and turned his head. Prunty came right back with a left jab and then his roundhouse right, while Hodges landed a left in Prunty's teeth again.

Both men backed off. Prunty looked grotesque with his pale forehead, squinting eyes, and bloody mouth. He was wheezing through his nose, but he was not breathing hard.

Hodges had his head lowered and his mouth open, but his guard was up.

"C'mon," he said again, motioning, as if he had been directing the fight all along.

Prunty came at him again, seeming never to tire of swinging the big right. This time Hodges ducked under the blow and reached his arms out. He closed in on Prunty and got his arms around Prunty's midsection.

As Hodges pushed forward and up, Prunty pushed downward in a sprawl. He hammered on the broad back and kidney area, and then he went straight up as Hodges lifted and squeezed.

Prunty's toes were still on the ground, so he still had some power. He kicked his feet back and pushed downward again, his chest on Hodges's left shoulder; then he hooked his right arm between his body and the other man's, locking onto Hodges's left arm. With another downward shove, he broke Hodges's grasp.

It was evident that Hodges wanted to get the fight down on the ground, where he could get his weight on top of Prunty. He stayed in close, still pushing, and reached again around Prunty's waist. Prunty hooked the arm and pushed downward again, and then both men came up. Prunty still had the arm hooked with his right. He threw his left forearm across Hodges's mouth and nose, which knocked Hodges's head back, and then he got both arms around the big man's waist. It looked like an iron band locking around the large midsection. Putting his hip into it, Prunty lifted the heavy man off the ground. Felver saw a pair of boots dangle in the air, and then Prunty slammed Hodges to the ground.

Felver heard a thud and then a soft, farty sound. Prunty stood back, but the man on the ground didn't move.

"Had enough?" said Prunty in a rasping voice.

Hodges said nothing, but he got up onto all fours, facing away from all the other men.

"Looks like he's had enough, Bill," said Dalhart.

Prunty had his mouth open, and his teeth were red. It looked as if he had cut his lip against his teeth. His pale forehead was flushed, and he was breathing hard. He said nothing more as he went to his hat and vest and put them on.

Felver looked at Carter, who was on his feet now. "I suppose that's enough," Felver said. "We didn't come here to fight, but that's the way it turned out."

Carter gave a glowering look at Prunty. "Well, it's not goin' to get him his money back."

Felver gave Carter a sharp look. "How do you know it was money?"

"I don't," said Carter, with some of his impudence returning. "Everyone knows he's a miser, though."

Felver looked at Prunty, who had his back to

the others as he hunched forward and buttoned his vest. Felver looked back at Carter. "You still haven't given us a straight answer about what you were doing up north about a week before all the stuff turned up missing."

"You didn't get the answer you wanted," answered Carter. "If you haven't beat it out of us by now, do you think you will?"

Felver looked at Hodges, who had turned over and was sitting on the ground. "Probably not," Felver said. He looked at Dalhart, who twisted his mouth and nodded. He looked around for Prunty, but the lean man was walking toward his horse, which had run about fifty yards out from the camp. "I guess that's it for today, then," Felver said. He led his horse out a few steps and mounted up. He looked back to see if either of the upstarts had gone near a gun, but neither had. "See you later," he said, watching them as Dalhart mounted his horse.

As Felver rode away from the camp, he didn't like having his back to the other two, but he didn't think they would try anything at this point. He glanced at Dalhart, who gave a small shake of the head as if to say there was no worry. They rode ahead, catching up with Prunty just as he was gathering his reins.

"Are you all right, Bill?" asked Dalhart.

Prunty nodded but did not open his mouth.

After they had ridden about half a mile, Dalhart said, "You thumped 'em both pretty

191

good, Bill." Getting no response, he turned to Felver. "Didn't he, though?"

"He sure did," Felver replied. "We didn't get any straight answers, but we probably weren't going to, anyway."

They rode on a little farther, and Dalhart spoke again. "You know," he said, "I believe they got a surprise, especially that fat one. Didn't it look like that to you, Felver?"

"Yes, it did."

Dalhart looked back at Prunty, who had fallen in behind them again. "What do you think, Bill?"

Prunty's voice was low and strained as he said, "I don't care."

They rode along for another mile until Felver spoke. "It's hard not to think that they're the ones that did it."

"Yeh," said Dalhart, "but short of searchin' 'em, which we don't have the right to do, I don't know how you could prove it."

"That's true. It seems we've gone about as far as we can go, then, doesn't it?"

"I suppose so. It's not much to take back to the boss, but it's something."

They rode through town and stopped only long enough to water their horses. Out on the west edge of town, Felver stopped his horse.

"What's wrong?" asked Dalhart.

"I just feel like we're not done, but I don't know what there is left to do."

Dalhart scratched his chin. "I don't, either."

"Well, I'll tell you what. I don't see any point in me goin' all the way back out to the ranch. How about if I stay here, and maybe some time around dark I'll go see if those boys are up to anything."

Dalhart shrugged. "I don't see anything wrong with that. Do you, Bill?"

Prunty shook his head.

"Well, so long, then," said Dalhart. "We'll report to the boss, and maybe catch up with you again tomorrow."

"Good enough. See you both later." Felver headed on west, while Dalhart and Prunty rode northwest.

Back at his camp, Felver thought everything looked normal. He had been gone two days, but the camp looked just as it did when he left. Inside the tent, everything was the same also. His rifle was still inside his blankets, and his warbag hadn't been disturbed. He hadn't really expected to lose anything. Aside from the small rash of thefts up north, he didn't know of people stealing from one another in this country. As a general rule, someone might steal cattle or horses, but they would leave a camp alone.

He unsaddled the horse and put it out to graze. After washing his face in the creek, he found some shade at the edge of the choke-cherry bushes and sat down to think.

Something Dalhart said came back to him. It was the part about searching them. Now that he thought of it, he imagined Hodges and Carter didn't have any of the goods. They would already have sold them to someone who had an outlet. That way, they could be brazen about it. They had an alibi, and they didn't have any of the evidence on them.

Felver stared at the tips of his boots. Hell, it was clear as day, or at least it could be. Coper gave them an alibi before the crimes, and he left town shortly afterward. He could easily have taken a satchel of loot with him. Felver shook his head. Maybe that was too easy an explanation. Why would Coper want to traffic with two-bit thieves? Why would he have to get money that way? He was a prosperous businessman, and it didn't cost that much to take care of the tent in his pants. Felver looked at his boots again. If three things happened in a row, that didn't mean they were related.

He looked up at the sun, which was almost straight up. It was a long time until dark, and he didn't have much to eat in the meanwhile. He remembered the steak he had eaten for breakfast, and he thought of the whole beef that Clarence said was hanging. It seemed silly for him to go into town and buy fresh meat when there were hundreds of pounds of it waiting to spoil. He wrinkled his nose and wondered why he always thought so much about food. He realized it was because he was hungry. That was simple enough. He could ride into town and buy some bacon; maybe the grease would be good for him. He laughed. If he got something to eat, he could think about other matters for a while.

He rode into town, bought a three-pound slab of bacon, and rode back. For the next hour he worked at building a fire, mixing dough, slicing bacon, and tending to the skillet and Dutch oven. He set a pot of coffee on the edge of the fire, and then his dinner was ready. Although he was hungry, he did not wolf his food. Enjoy a meal while he could, he thought.

When he had cleaned up after the meal, he went into the tent to lie down for a little while. The afternoon shadows were starting to creep out, and he thought he might as well rest while he had a chance.

He awoke with a start. Everything was gray inside the tent. He couldn't remember if it was morning or evening. He still had his boots on. Crawling out of the tent, he stood up and looked around. He went to the fire pit, crouched, and held his hand over the ashes of the campfire. Heat was still rising. He remembered the bacon and biscuits. Putting his hand on the coffeepot, he could feel it was still warm.

He walked out to his horse and saw the sun slipping in the western sky. It was sure enough evening, just as he had thought.

Back at camp, he poured himself a cup of lukewarm coffee and squatted on his heels to drink it. He needed to make himself get up and move around. He had slept too heavily.

Then he remembered he was supposed to go check on the other camp. He hurried out to get the horse, saddled it in an instant, and hit the trail. Rather than go through town, he crossed the creek and struck off across country. He loped the horse for about a mile, then slowed it to a trot. If Hodges and Carter were in camp, they would have a fire, and he would see it from a ways off. If they weren't, he might find them in town.

He had a good idea of where he was headed, although he was approaching the camp from a different direction now. At about the place he expected, he saw the clump of trees. No fire flickered in their midst, and no smell of wood smoke floated on the air.

Coming at the camp from the west, he thought he would ride past it just to be sure he was in the right place. He wouldn't go in and snoop around, no matter how much he might feel tempted. It was dusk now, and light was fading. He saw the worn area in the middle of the camp, then the broken glass in the trash heap, and the scraps of paper beyond that. He stopped the horse and looked closer. The black deer carcass still hung in the tree, and the jagged firewood still lay in a heap on the other side of the fire pit. Otherwise, the camp was empty. Hodges and Carter had pulled out.

Chapter Eleven

Felver could not imagine Hodges and Carter pulling out because of the encounter earlier in the day. The two young upstarts had gotten a good drubbing at the hands of Prunty, but they wouldn't have let that run them off. Similarly, they had had some uncomfortable questions put to them, but that would probably not have caused them to leave their camp either. Felver thought they were brazen enough to endure embarrassment and suspicion, especially with the help of a few brave swigs and the assumption that it would all blow over.

It was more probable, he thought, that they had gone into town to take a room and have their weekly bath. Now that night was falling, they were probably either sitting in the Doubloon or on their way there.

By the time Felver rode into town, night had closed in. He rode his horse to the patch of light in front of the Doubloon. He didn't recognize any of the horses as belonging to Hodges and Carter, but that didn't mean anything. If they had come to town to put up in a room, they would probably have stabled their horses.

Felver tied his horse at the hitch rack and stepped up to the doorway of the Doubloon. Three men, all unknown to him, stood at the

197

bar. No one sat at the tables. Felver walked down the sidewalk and stepped in for a quick peek in the café. He planned to come back later to see Jenny, so he just looked long enough to verify that he didn't know anyone seated at the tables. Next he went to the Blue Horse Saloon, and there also he saw no one he knew. He was not surprised that Hodges and Carter were not there, as he did not recall ever having seen them in the place. On the other hand, he thought it unusual not to see either Heid or McNair, as they were usually holding forth before sundown. It occurred to him that all four young men might be at the same place, perhaps at some event that held their common interest, such as a card game or a steak feed.

Felver ordered a beer at the bar, and when it came, he asked the barkeep if there was anything going on in town that evening. The bartender said that, no, there wasn't. Things were pretty dead, especially for a Saturday night. He asked Felver what sort of sport he was looking for. Felver said he didn't have anything in mind.

"This is as lively as it gets in this town," said the bartender, with a sweep of the arm. "At least for the time being."

Felver drank his beer and gave the situation a little thought. He didn't have any business with Hodges and Carter even if he found them, but he thought he would have a better grasp of things if he knew where they were. As for Heid and McNair, he still thought that either or both of them might shed more light on Coper and his affairs.

Knowing that Jenny would be getting off work before long, he did not dawdle over his beer. He drank it while it was still cold, but he did not drink it too fast to enjoy it.

Back out on the sidewalk, after noting a dim light still burning in the kitchen area of the café, he sat on the bench and appreciated the cool evening air. The smell of dust and manure and horse sweat was never far away in this world, but it was an easy, familiar world. When a fellow had the leisure to sit on a bench in a slow, quiet place, life seemed innocent enough. Maybe some fellows had stolen some things, but he, Felver, had just had a pleasant mug of beer and was waiting for a girl.

As he waited, he thought about how different he had felt the last couple of times he had seen her, as compared with the first few encounters. When he had first seen her, he thought she might be a bit low-class but worth a tumble or two. Now he appreciated her self-respect, her sense of propriety. She had gone into the tent with him, but she had gone in and come out with dignity. Open and honest, she had looked him in the face and had told him she trusted him. She had let him into her world, which was trust in itself, and now she trusted him with having done it. That was how he saw it — she trusted him with their confidentiality, their intimacy. He thought there was a natural decency to her being that way and to her being able to tell him. She no doubt knew what it was like to be vulnerable, to be exploited after having let someone in, so if she trusted him, it wasn't because she didn't know any better.

· She had said she wasn't a bad girl, and he believed it. He could remember his reaction, pure reflex, when someone — Heid once and Carter another time — had been on the verge of a slur. Something had kicked inside him both times. It was the feeling that, in spite of appearances, she was a decent woman who deserved respect.

He had no doubt that he wanted to get close to her again, but he felt his motives were decent. It wasn't something he wanted to do all by itself. It was something he wanted to do so things would develop between them. She wasn't a stranger, totally outside him, as she had been before. She had grown into him, as he imagined he had done with her, and he wanted to have more of a shared world with her.

Maybe that was what had changed, he thought. He used to see her as a different kind of person, as if he and she were different kinds of creatures, and now he saw that they probably weren't. It wasn't just a matter of class, although he had had to think through that by degrees as well, agreeing with himself that they both worked, they both got dirty and sweaty, and they both did natural things. Deeper than that, he now felt they were the same kind of animal, with the same kind of blood and the same feelings. It wasn't on an animal level, but it was. A jackrabbit couldn't breed with a cottontail because they were just different by nature. What was on the physical level with the rabbits was on the feeling level with him and her. That was the best way he could explain it to himself. They weren't different by nature.

A loud voice from the Blue Horse Saloon brought him back to the present moment. She should be coming out pretty soon, and if he could judge by the nervous feeling in his stomach, she had become a fuller person to him than she was the first day he had met her here on this sidewalk.

When the door latch finally sounded and she stepped out into the night, he stood up and said, "Good evening." As he spoke, he realized he had taken off his hat.

"Hello," she said. "I was hoping you'd come into town before long."

"Actually, I was in town yesterday, but I was on the job and was with a couple of other hands, so I didn't stop in. We ended up having to leave on short order, as this one old fellow, the cook, got into a little ruckus and we had to take him home."

"You're not on the job now, then?" She started walking toward the hotel.

He put on his hat as he fell in beside her. "No, not exactly. I'm sort of keepin' a lookout for those two troublemakers. In fact, they're the ones old Clarence had the run-in with, and then they had a tangle with another fellow from the ranch, name of Prunty. I'm all but sure that they're the ones who pulled those jobs up north, and I'm wonderin' where they are and what they're up to."

"I haven't seen them in town today, and I don't remember if I saw them yesterday."

"Well, if they're gone, it's good riddance, but they're more likely around somewhere, and up to no good." Felver and Jenny walked along the sidewalk for a ways in silence until he spoke. "Everything about the same with you?"

"Oh, yes. It's just work and sleep and kill time. About the only thing that keeps me going is the idea that I'm going to get out of that joint."

He gave her his hand as they stepped off the sidewalk for a cross street. "If you had your choice," he said, "what would you do next?"

"Just start over," she said without hesitation. "Just go somewhere else where I'm not labeled from the beginning." She put a little pressure on his hand as she stepped up onto the next sidewalk. "You know, I don't mind working. I just don't like to be treated like something . . . left over." She glanced at him as they walked past a lit window.

"That shouldn't be so hard," he said. "Just get a ways away from the place — or the people in this place, I should say."

She let out a sigh. "It sounds easy just to say

it. But when you're stuck in a place, it's hard to get out. You need the money for the fare or whatever, for the food and lodging, and then to get set up in the next place."

"Well, it might not be so bad if you've got someone to go it with you." He looked at her, and she nodded. "For example," he went on, "if you had enough to get a horse, I could get us to the next place, and then you could decide if you want to go your own way or whatever, and you'd still have the horse to sell."

They came to the patch of light outside the Doubloon. Felver paused long enough to see the same three men as before, then continued the walk.

"It wouldn't be like we were on the bum," she said.

"Oh, no. I've got a good-enough camp outfit, and the travel wouldn't cost much. And then when we got there, I'd have enough for either one or both of us to put up in a decent place."

"Oh, uh-huh."

He hoped she understood that in sharing expenses, she would have a chance at recovering hers. "Anyway, that's one way it could be done."

They walked on for a ways, crossed another side street, and approached the hotel. "Then," she said, "if you wanted to get loose of me, you could."

He smiled. "Or the other way. You might know me well enough by then that you'll be ready to get rid of me."

"I don't think I'll feel that way," she said.

"I hope not, but you never know. And you ought to at least have the chance for a say-so."

She stopped before they came to the light outside the hotel. "So you're saying there wouldn't be any assumptions on either side."

"It could work that way. If either one of us wanted to call it good at that point, well, then no one would feel trapped."

"Suppose we went to a place like Laramie," she said. "I wouldn't want to go back to Cheyenne. But suppose we went to another place, and you didn't want to stay."

He shrugged. "Well, I sure wouldn't do it in such a way as to make you look bad. I would make sure you had a place on your own, to put you back on your feet for the time being. But to tell you the truth, I hope that wherever we go, neither of us wants to call it quits. I just wouldn't want you to feel that you couldn't get out if you wanted to." He held his hands out, and she took them in hers.

"It seems . . . gallant of you, Owen."

"Well, I don't know if that's overstatin' it, but it's how a girl makes a fella feel."

"It makes me feel good, too," she said.

He leaned toward her for a quick kiss. "I still don't know how long the boss might keep me around, but I don't think it'll be for long."

"Well, just don't leave without telling me

first," she said, forming her lips in a playful pout.

"I won't."

She hesitated, then said, "Well, I suppose I should go on in. Are you going to the ranch now?"

"Um, no. Actually, I'm going back to my camp. If I don't hear from Dalhart by this time tomorrow, then maybe I'll go out to the ranch then."

"Oh, I see."

"I'm glad you mentioned it. I'd want you to know where I was, and of course I'd want you to know my camp is always open."

She paused as she glanced in the direction of the hotel. "I don't think I would feel good about going right now."

He felt his optimism sinking, so he said quickly, "You could come out in the morning. I've got something for breakfast, and I've always got coffee."

She considered for another moment and then said, "I could do that. It seems like the best time for me to get away."

"Do you want me to come for you?"

"Oh, no," she said. "It's a nice walk that early in the morning — and besides, you'll be busy in the kitchen."

"That's right," he said.

They came together for a quick kiss and then parted. He stood and watched as she walked away toward the entrance of the hotel. He waved when she turned to wave at him, and then when she was gone into the hotel, he stepped down into the street and took brisk, light steps back to his horse.

It was a calm night as he led the horse into the middle of the street and mounted up. He didn't feel a need to check the saloons again. He would just ride back to his camp and get a good night's sleep. As he rode out of town, he saw that some houses lay in darkness while others had light behind the curtained windows. Once again he wondered which house was Coper's.

In the morning, Felver washed his face in the creek and enjoyed the cool, clear feeling that the water gave. His skin felt fresh, and his eyes felt more open than before. It was as if he took in the new morning with his hands, his face, his eyes — all the parts that were not covered by clothing and that now had yesterday washed away.

As he walked past the chokecherry trees, he saw that the clusters of small fruit were turning color from green to red. It would be a while yet, probably ten days or two weeks, until the little cherries turned dark. When they were almost black, and soft to the touch, that was the time to strip off a handful and eat them, mashing the pulp and separating the pits, then spitting them out. Chokecherries were juicy, but they also left a dry, puckery taste that called for water. A fellow would have to eat a long time to make any part of a meal with them, but they were pleasurable to eat. He imagined he would be off somewhere else by the time these got ripe, but for all he knew, he might be in a place where other black, shiny clusters would hang within his reach.

He started a fire, took his horse to water, and got the coffeepot ready. He mixed dough for drop biscuits, then sliced bacon for the skillet. He could see the sun filtering through the cotton-wood trees, but it had not yet cleared the tops when Jenny appeared at the edge of the grove. She waved, and he walked out to meet her.

She was wearing her light blue dress, so she looked fresh as he walked toward her. The color reminded him of blue flax, which put on new blooms each morning. Her hair looked clean, as did her face, and her eyes had a sparkle that went nicely with the blue dress. He touched his left hand to her right, then took off his hat so he could lean in to kiss her.

"Nice morning," he said. "How was your walk?"

"Oh, just fine. It doesn't take long at all to get here."

They walked back to the campsite, where he made her a seat out of folded canvas sheets and packs. Then he set the skillet and the coffeepot on the coals.

"You get along pretty well this way, don't you?" she said.

"Oh, it's an easy way to be when you're foot-loose, just goin' from one place to another, but you couldn't do it forever. At least, I couldn't."

"I suppose."

"In bad weather, for example. A fellow wants a bunkhouse or a cabin, if not a regular house, when winter sets in." He smiled at her. "You get wind and snow and a deep freezin' cold, and you want to be in a snug place."

She smiled back. "You don't mind living in a house, then, or inside."

"Oh, no, not at all. There's some company better than others." He thought of the two nights he had spent in the bunkhouse amid Prunty's wheezing and Clarence's snoring, and then he thought about what it would be like to sleep next to the soft, gentle presence of a woman like her. "If a person could choose, it could be downright enjoyable."

She blushed. "Have you ever lived with a woman?"

He shook his head as he poked at the bacon with his knife. "No, but I've lived in bunk-houses and work camps with a lot of different men, and I've got some idea of what a fella would choose not to be around."

She gave a light laugh. "I've heard married women say you don't really know what a man is like until you're married to him and you have to live with him. And of course, at that point, you can't choose not to."

He raised his eyebrows as he moved the

bacon in the skillet. "I imagine so. And I think it works the other way, too."

She laughed harder this time. "Oh, yes, I'm sure of that. My brother married a real daisy. She was sweet as pie until she had her first baby, and then she got fat and contrary."

He laughed at her and grinned. "You wouldn't do that, would you?"

She laughed, almost in a giggle. "I hope not. She's a fright."

They chatted on as the bacon sizzled and the coffeepot sent out plumes of steam. Somewhere across the creek in the grass, a meadowlark tinkled its silvery clear song on the morning air.

They ate their breakfast and enjoyed another cup of coffee. Felver thought Jenny was a good girl, eating a line camp breakfast as cheerfully as if it were ham and eggs back home. With the coffee, also, she didn't flinch, handling the hot tin cup as if it were an everyday household cup.

The sun rose above the cottonwoods and warmed the morning, driving away the coolness. Felver could feel perspiration form where his shirt touched his neck.

"Might get warm," he said.

She blinked and nodded, then covered her mouth as she stifled a yawn. "You know what I'd like to do?"

"What's that?"

"I'd like to go wading in the creek. I haven't done that in a long time."

Felver looked at his boots. He remembered enjoying it when he had walked barefoot through the creek in this same place a couple of weeks earlier. "Shouldn't be much trouble," he said, "and there's nobody around to bother us."

She looked around and shook her head. "Looks fine to me."

"I'm game," he said. He turned around to have his back to her as he took off his boots and socks. Then he turned back. Her dark blue stockings lay draped over her shoes, and her pale white feet showed below the hem of her dress. He stood up and offered her his hand.

When she stood up next to him, they met in a brief kiss. Then they walked to the creek, which was less than a foot deep. She raised her dress as she stepped into the water, showing her slender ankles. Felver bent over to cuff up his trousers, and then he stepped into the water beside her.

The water felt cold on his feet when he first stepped in, but after a couple of minutes it just felt cool and clean.

Still clutching her dress with both hands, Jenny stepped back and forth and side to side in the water. She smiled as she looked down.

"How do you like it?" he asked.

"It's really a pleasure." She looked at him and smiled.

He smiled back without speaking.

"It's funny," she said. "There's not much you can do like this, but it sure gives you the feeling of being free."

"That's true." He stepped closer to her and put his hand on her shoulder. As she made a half-turn to him, he put both hands on her waist and leaned to kiss her as she, with both hands still holding the skirt of her dress, gave him back his kiss.

They released, and he looked down at her bare feet and ankles. He moved his right foot over to play with her feet. She looked at him and smiled, then put her right foot on top of his. When both of them stood flat-footed again on the gravel bed of the creek, he held her and kissed her once more.

"It's nice not to have any mosquitoes at this time of day," he said, relaxing as he stood facing her with his hands at his side.

She gave a shy smile. "I haven't forgotten about them."

He looked at her feet and moved his right foot in a swirl above them. "You've got pretty feet."

"Well, thank you."

He felt a mischievous smile play upon his face. "Have you thought about how you might get back over to the camp without getting them dirty?"

She glanced toward the camp. "Well, no, I haven't." Her eyes met his as she said, "I suppose you have."

"Yes, I have. I figure I can just pick you up and carry you over there."

"Oh, do you think you could?" She gave him a little frown.

"I know I can. You just have to grab on to me so you don't fall."

"You're sure, aren't you?"

"You bet I am. You just tell me when."

She looked at her feet. "Well, I guess this is good enough for right now."

"Well, let's try." He moved toward her, dropping his right arm behind her knees as he held his left hand behind her head. She put her arms around his neck as he lifted her, with feet dripping, above the creek.

Her eyes were close to his and full of fun. "Don't you drop me now, Owen. You hear?"

"Not a chance," he said, snugging his hold on her. "You're perfect this way, and I wouldn't want to spoil it." He carried her to the campsite, and seeing the tent flap open, he said, "Do you want me to set you in the shade there, inside the tent?"

She turned her head and said, "That would be all right."

He had to bunch himself up to duck into the tent and get her seated, but he managed it. He was kneeling next to her, with his eyes at her level. Leaning forward and closing his eyes, he felt his lips meet hers. Then they both settled down to lie together on his bedding.

As they lay in their embrace, kissing, he moved his hand upon her without restraint or hurry. She had her hand on his hip and was not holding him away, so he caressed her as he had done before. She responded with gentle motion.

He was kissing her on the neck now, and on the fabric that covered her breasts. Moving his hand from her ribs to her calves, he fumbled at her dress and felt awkward. "I wouldn't know how to take this off you if you thought it was a thing to do."

Her voice was soft as she said, "I'll do it."

He looked away and heard the rustle of clothing. Then he heard and felt her lie down as she said, in her soft voice, "Okay."

In a moment of magic he turned and saw her, undressed and reclined like a goddess. Everything was consistent, from her pretty, well-shaped feet and ankles all the way to her nicely featured face. Her soft, pale body looked flawless in the muted light inside the tent. He wanted to caress her all at once, to kiss and adore her perfect texture, but he felt vulgar in his clothes. He did not want to start, then stop to take off his clothes, then start again. He didn't want to spoil the magic.

"Just a minute," he said. He turned again and took off his clothes, restraining himself from seeming too hurried.

He lay next to her, their bodies touching. Again he had the feeling that he and she were the same, not different by nature but matched to each other, the same in body and blood. They weren't the same person, but they were the same kind of person, inside and out.

A few minutes later, her eyes looked up into his as he still lay on top of her. The blue eyes were sparkling, and she had a soft smile on her face.

"It's better this way, isn't it?" she said.

At first he thought she meant in the light rather than in the dark, and then he thought she meant with all of their clothes off. Either way, or both, she was right. "It sure is," he agreed.

They lay side by side for a few minutes without saying anything, until Jenny spoke.

"You know what I've always wanted to do?"

He looked into her eyes. "What?"

"I've always wanted to lie in the sun with nothing on, to feel the sunlight all over me."

Felver remembered the feeling from having done it himself. "Oh, uh-huh," he said, looking at her and meeting her eyes with his.

"Can we?"

"You mean, take the bedding outside?"

She nodded. "Yes. Just for a few minutes. To see what it feels like."

He realized she had the same appreciation of pleasure as he did. "Sure," he said.

Within a few minutes he had the bedding laid out in the sunlight between the tent and the chokecherry bushes. He didn't expect anybody at this time of day, but he thought the tent and the bushes would give a sense of protection.

The two of them reclined together in the morning sunlight, stretching and relaxing and then turning to face each other. He put his right arm beneath her head, and then they fell into another long kiss, caressing each other with their free hands. They drew apart and continued to touch and pet for several minutes. He admired all of her, seeing her even more like a perfect goddess in the open light of day.

He felt the sun on his back as he nestled upon her breast, with her hand at the back of his head. In a little while they were face-to-face, length-to-length, and he could feel the warm sun all the way down his back, from his shoulders to his calves. He had a feeling of total freedom. The world stretched out in all directions — water, dirt, grass, rock, tree, sky, and sun. Nothing enclosed him; nothing held him down. It was as if he was expanding in all directions.

He thought she might like to feel that way, too. Slowing his motion, he said, "Don't you think you'd like to feel the sun on your back?"

Her blue eyes were open. "Right now?"

"Sure."

"Well, I guess we can try."

They separated and changed positions, and soon they found their new motion. Felver could hear the trickle of the creek, and above him he could see the red fruit on the chokecherry branches, and beyond that the blue sky and a white cloud. He closed his eyes and tucked his head close to hers.

"I haven't ever done it this way," she whispered.

"Neither have I," he whispered back. Her buttocks were sun-warm to the touch. "It comes naturally, though, doesn't it?"

"Yes," she said, covering his face with her flowing hair as she joined her lips to his in a long, wet kiss.

Afterward, as they enjoyed the free sunlight a while longer, Felver had a sense of the world coming back in around him. There were other people in the world, he remembered. He thought that most of them, even if they had caught a glance from a mile off, would have the decency to look away. A man had a right to his own camp and what went on there. Still, he began to feel self-conscious.

"What would you think about going back into the tent?" he asked.

She stretched her head forward to look at her abdomen. "It's probably a good idea. I don't want to get a sunburn."

Back in the tent, she began to get dressed. Felver appreciated her movement, which seemed simple and graceful to him, and he had a renewed sense of her dignity as she made herself presentable to the world again. He dressed himself then, and when he was finished he saw that she was, too.

"It was nice to have the sun and the sky all to ourselves, wasn't it?" he asked.

Her smile was tender. "Oh, yes, it was. I'll remember it." She looked outside the tent and said, "Owen, would you be a darling and bring me my shoes and stockings?"

He looked at her pretty feet and ankles, then leaned and kissed her left ankle, which was nearest him. As his eyes met hers he said, "Sure. Anything to be a darling."

He fetched his own boots and socks at the same time, and he pulled his on in short order. When she had her shoes and stockings back on, he stood outside the tent and gave her his hand. She stood up straight, the sun shining on her clear features. She brushed her hair back, then lowered her hands to meet his.

"I hate to think about going back to town, but I probably should."

"Well, let's hope it's just for a short while."

She nodded. "I hope so."

As they met in a soft kiss and embrace, he felt the closeness of their bodies. They seemed to belong together. They weren't at all different by nature. Except that she looked like a goddess at some moments, they were quite the same.

Chapter Twelve

The man from Wolf River drank from the mug of cold beer the bartender had set before him. The beer tasted good in his mouth and throat, and the pleasing sensation spread outward. After a good night's sleep, a hearty breakfast, some cozy cuddling, and now a cold beer, a man felt at peace with the world — even if, for the moment, the center of the world was the empty Blue Horse Saloon at midafternoon. Felver knew better than to drink more than one beer by himself on a hot day, but he could allow himself that much of an indulgence.

After escorting Jenny to town, Felver had gone back to his camp and waited. When Dalhart hadn't shown up by midday, Felver had eaten the leftovers from breakfast and had gone back to town. To combine business and pleasure, he had gone to the Blue Horse Saloon. Now he sat in the empty barroom, which was dark along the walls and corners but had good light coming in through the door. He did not expect to see Heid and McNair at such an early hour, but he thought he should take some initiative rather than sit around and wait, and he thought he could at least ask a few questions here.

"Where are those young sports Heid and

McNair?" he asked the bartender, who had returned to his stool behind the bar.

"I couldn't say. I'd guess Heid is out of town. That's the only reason I could imagine for him not comin' in yesterday. Now McNair, he did come in, but it was later on." The bartender, who had been cleaning his fingernails with a penknife, looked up and asked, "Are you lookin' for 'em?"

Felver was quite sure the bartender had recognized him each time he had been in since that first day when he had ridden his horse up to the doorway, so he imagined the bartender recalled seeing him with Heid and McNair. "Not really. It's just that I've been in here a couple of times at this time of day, and I've sat around and passed the time with them."

The bartender yawned. "Oh, they usually come in a little later. Like I said, Heid didn't come in yesterday, and that's not like him if he's in town."

"Oh, uh-huh." Felver sipped on his beer. He thought it odd that Heid would be out of circulation at the same time that Hodges and Carter had become scarce.

The bartender shifted the penknife into his left hand and continued cleaning his fingernails. He was a tall, dark-haired man about thirty, a little pale in the face and soft around the middle. With an air of worldly wisdom about him, he did not answer Felver's brief response.

"Well, they're pretty cheerful young sports," Felver offered.

"That they are. There's lots of times they're the only life in here."

"One thing I never did catch," said Felver, "is where it is that McNair lives."

"You'd think he lived under a bridge, but what with there not bein' a bridge anywhere near here, he stays in the watchman's shack down at the stock pens."

"Oh, I didn't know he worked." Felver drank from his beer.

"It's not so much that he works, seein' as how there's hardly ever any stock in the pens until shippin' time, but insofar as they need someone who sleeps in the daytime, he fills the bill."

Felver recalled seeing the stock pens on the east side of town, south of the main street and edging up to the creek. He hadn't seen any livestock in the pens, and he did not remember having seen any signs of life. For all he knew, McNair could have been there, sleeping, when he rode by. "I suppose things get pretty busy here at shippin' time," he said.

"Oh, somewhat. But if anyone brings stock to town, it's just for overnight until they can move it on." The bartender stood up and brushed off his lap. "What this town needs is a railroad. Then all these cattlemen could ship their steers from right here, and spend their money right here. And you'd get freight in here a hell of a lot easier, too."

"Might be hard on anyone who's got a drayage company."

The bartender shrugged. "You look at any town that's got a railroad, and you'll see more business there. More saloons, more eatin' houses — you name it."

Felver thought of McNair's joke. "Parlors."

"Them too. Where there's railroads, there's crib girls."

"What's the chance?" Felver took another drink.

"Of a railroad comin' here? Pretty slim. But that's what's buildin' this country, is the railroads."

Still thinking of McNair, Felver thought a railroad town would be a good place for that young man. "Sometimes you wonder how people end up in a town like this."

The bartender shrugged as he sat back down on his stool. "For lack of a better place, I guess. Some folks might fool themselves and think they come to make money, but they find out soon enough there's not much money to be had here."

Felver had a fleeting image of Coper. "Oh, it seems like there's always someone who's got a little bit — at least more than the rest of us."

"I don't think anyone in this town has got any money to speak of."

"I hardly know anyone here," said Felver, "but I thought there might be someone, say a businessman, who might be a little better off and could throw ice-cream socials and such."

"Might be," said the bartender, "but when people of that nature can't even pay for their own groceries, you know they're not that far ahead of the rest of us."

Felver sensed that the bartender was warming up to the sharing of knowledge. "Oh, I didn't know," he said as he tipped up his mug.

"That's a small town for you. When a man charges the storekeeper to freight in some grub, and then turns around and takes his own groceries on credit, the word gets around."

Felver pursed his lips. "Is that hard cheese on Mr. Heid?"

The bartender snapped his knife shut. "I don't know yet. I might when bills come due at the end of the month." He looked at Felver's mug. "Care for another one?"

Felver sensed that the bartender had said as much as he was going to say for the present. He tipped his mug to drink the last of his beer, then said, "Not right now, thanks. I've got a couple of things to look after."

Outside, he was glad he hadn't drunk any more. The sun was bright, and the afternoon was hot. Felver had the feeling that everything had come to a standstill. Hodges and Carter had dropped out of view, Heid was off somewhere, and McNair was probably just greeting the day. Dalhart hadn't come back, either, and Felver thought something ought to be happening pretty soon or else the whole business might blow over after all.

He decided to pursue the one lead that seemed feasible at the moment. Untying his horse and gathering the reins, he swung into the saddle and headed for the stock pens.

As he approached the pens, they looked as he remembered them — empty and nondescript. He saw the shack, which he hadn't had any reason to notice before. Small and weathered and not much bigger than a two-seat outhouse, it lay at the southwest corner of the pens. Felver did not see any signs of life, nor did he hear any after he called out. Dismounting, he rapped his knuckles on the door. Still no answer came. He swung into the saddle and rode back into town.

It occurred to him that he could check on his packhorse at the livery stable. While he was at it, he might pick up a hint about the comings and goings of Hodges and Carter or of Heid. The livery stable lay at the other end of town, past Five Star Drayage and on the same side of the street. Felver did not see any activity up ahead outside Coper's business, but he saw a freight wagon in front of the mercantile store, which also sat on the north side of the street, a block before he would pass the drayage office.

As he approached the freight wagon, Felver recognized the two freighters who had delivered the building materials. Dalhart had said they could lift a piano. Right now they were lowering a dark drum of what Felver imagined to be kerosene. They were lowering the barrel down a ramp by means of a parbuckle, a rope sling fastened to the tail end of the wagon and looped around the ends of the drum. The men were paying out the two lengths of rope to let the barrel roll slowly down the ramp. They were making smooth work of their task, and they did not pay any attention to Felver as he rode by.

He did not look at the drayage company as he rode past, and he was relieved that no one stepped out of the shadows to call his name. He rode on to the livery stable, where he watered his horse and chatted with the stable man. Felver asked the man if he had any idea of where Heid might be.

With no apparent attempt at humor, the stable man said, "I haven't seen hide nor hair of him." He leaned to spit out through the doorway. "But that queer duck friend of his came a little while ago and borrowed his horse. He said he had Heid's permission, and I figgered if he didn't he'd catch hell from Heid, and what with them bein' so thick, I let him take it."

"Oh, I doubt there's much harm done."

"Nah, I doubt it."

"He didn't say where Heid was, though, did he?"

"No, he didn't. He just said he was gone — and of course that he'd given him permission."

Felver nodded, thanked the stable man, and told him he would probably be back in a day or two to pick up his packhorse. Without a definite plan, he mounted his horse and headed back to the middle of town. As the horse took its slow steps, Felver recalled Dalhart's remark that McNair didn't have a horse, and he wondered what use the queer duck would have for one. Felver shrugged. Maybe it was none of his business. All the same, he thought it would be worth his while to sound out McNair.

Felver rode back through town and toward the stock pens. Now he saw a horse tied up outside the shack, a sorrel horse with a white blaze. He imagined McNair must have come back by way of a side street. Felver rode up to the shack and called out a greeting.

McNair appeared at the dark doorway, shading his eyes with his hand on the bill of his cap and looking out onto the bright afternoon. "What do you want?"

"Just dropped by to say hello. Thought maybe you could help me out on a little puzzle I'm workin' on."

"Depends on the puzzle, but come on in." McNair lowered his hand and turned back into the shack.

Felver dismounted, tied his horse next to the sorrel, and walked to the doorway. After a moment, his eyes adjusted to the dark interior, and he saw McNair sitting on a bunk with his cap tipped back on his head.

"Have a seat," said McNair, motioning toward a single chair that sat in the middle of the room.

Felver sat down. The shack was dark and dingy, and a smell of old clothes and cigarette smoke hung on the air. "Hope it's not a bother, my droppin' by like this."

McNair lifted a half-smoked cigarette to his mouth. "Not so much. I just don't get many visitors here."

Felver thought he would try to revive the wit of earlier conversations. "Maybe it's because you're out so much in society, and you make yourself available there."

"That must be it." McNair tapped the ash of his cigarette onto the floor. "So tell me what the puzzle is that you're workin' on."

Felver tipped back his hat. His vision was getting better, and he could see the yellowed cigarette stain on McNair's fingers. "Actually, it's the same one as before. Still tryin' to figure out who stole the valuables out of the ranch houses up north."

McNair's sunken eyes peered through a haze of smoke. "I don't know what I could tell you."

"Not to mention any names," said Felver, "but there's a couple young fellas that I can't get a straight answer out of. They say they were workin' for Coper, but that doesn't answer all the questions."

McNair ran the tip of his tongue out the corner of his mouth and then back in. "Not to mention any names, but you won't get any-thing straight out of some fellas."

"That's the way it seems. So I was wondering if there was any way you might shed some light on it."

McNair had leveled his gaze at Felver. "How do you think I might do that?"

Felver hesitated and then spoke. "Well, you know Heid, and Heid knows Coper, and Coper supposedly had these fellas on a job."

"I think he did." McNair hiked his right boot onto his left knee.

Felver found himself getting irritated at the same old runaround. "Then what the hell were they up north for, a week earlier?"

McNair gave a leer that showed his yellow teeth. He looked primitive as before, especially with the dark background of the unlit interior of the shack. "What do you think?" he asked.

Felver thought for a second. He couldn't see what he had to lose, so he said, "I think they might have been gettin' the lay of the land."

McNair took a drag on his cigarette. "And so?"

"And so I wonder why Coper is willing to say they were working for him."

"Maybe they were."

Felver let a short, heavy breath out of his nostrils. "Well, why would they be gettin' the lay of the land? To do those jobs. And how could they do those jobs if they were working for Coper?"

McNair put on a look of exaggerated inno-
cence as he took one last drag on the stub of
his cigarette. With the tips of his thumb and
forefinger, he tossed the stub onto the floor.
Then he ground it out with the heel of his
shoe.

A surge ran up the back of Felver's neck and
through his scalp. It was like he had thought.
The room swam for a moment until he shook
his head and phrased a clear question. "Why
would they be doing that kind of work for
him?"

McNair rubbed his thumb across the ends of
his first two fingers.

"Well, sure. That's why they'd be doing it.
But what I meant was, why would he have them
doing it?"

McNair raised his eyebrows and dropped the
corners of his mouth.

"Well, then, he really must be hard up."
Felver looked at McNair and realized that the
bitter young man had something to say as long
as he got to say it in his own way and in his
own good time. McNair was staring beyond
Felver now, as if he was deciding how much to
say. Maybe he was trying to figure out how to
tell on Coper without telling on Heid.

After a long moment, McNair spoke. "He
was too good to get his hands dirty himself."

"So he had someone else do the dirty work."

McNair had a look of contempt on his stone
face. "That's his way."

Felver had two questions, and he wasn't sure which one to ask first. He thought he needed to work from the outside in, so he asked what he thought was the outside question. "Why did they need to work for him? That is, why didn't they just steal for themselves?"

McNair held up his first and second fingers like rabbit ears. "Two reasons. One, he gave them an alibi, and two, he had an outlet for things that couldn't be turned into ready money around here."

"The trip to Denver."

"Exactly."

"I suppose he's back by now."

"That he is."

Felver brought out the second question. "Why would he have to do it, though?"

McNair, who had his lips set in an expression of distaste, said nothing.

"I imagine he was in trouble."

McNair looked past Felver again, and then he brought his sullen gaze back. "He was."

Felver thought it was starting to make sense now. "With Heid?" he asked.

McNair nodded, and his face was impassive again.

Felver decided to keep going until he got stopped. "Are they related? They both came from St. Louis, didn't they?"

"They did, but I don't think there's a relation."

Felver paused, not sure of which way to go

next. "Then why did Heid come out here?"

"It was on a lead. Someone made him think Coper was his father, and he hated him for the possibility."

"And he's been squeezin' him for money for that?"

"No. That was just what got him here. You asked why he came."

"Well, yes, I did. I supposed it had something to do with Coper being in trouble."

"Well, it does and it doesn't." McNair took out his tobacco and papers.

Felver thought McNair was still uncertain about how far to go. If McNair was trying to cover for Heid, then Felver could try to slant his questions from another angle so that they would be about Coper. "Was he in trouble because of something he did?"

McNair gave him a look that accused him of being stupid. "What else would it be?" Then he shook tobacco into his cigarette paper.

Felver decided not to take the sarcasm personally. "I guess what I mean is, was he in trouble for something he did and that someone knew he did?"

"That's hittin' it pretty close." McNair pulled the drawstring of the Bull Durham bag with his teeth.

Felver sensed that McNair wanted to tell him, so he went on. "Well, I guess I'll just have to ask in plain words. What did he do?"

McNair finished rolling his cigarette and

then lit it before he spoke. Shooting a quick cloud of smoke upward, he poked out his cheek with his tongue and then said, "He was looking in on a man and his wife doing something."

Felver flinched. "And Heid was shadowing him?"

McNair nodded and poked out his cheek again.

"That's pretty low."

"Which one?"

"Well, Coper. He's just a . . . Peeping Tom." Felver remembered the first time he had met Coper. He recalled how the well-dressed man had gotten flustered at Felver's offhand remark that he shouldn't go peeking in windows. So that was what he was — a low-down peeping Tom, just like Jenny thought. Felver shuddered. Coper wasn't just trying to look at girls when they took their clothes off. That was bad enough, but he wanted to see what went on between another man and woman.

· Felver remembered the pale, perfect skin, the pressure of her kiss, the red chokecherries and dark green leaves against a blue sky, the sighing and murmuring that belonged to just the two of them. In that moment of reflection he despised Coper. No one had a right to do that. Whether a man and a woman were married or otherwise, what went on between them was personal. They had a right to do as they pleased without having to worry about someone peeping through the keyhole or through a crack in the curtains.

Felver looked at McNair, who had lit his cigarette and seemed to be smoking it in vengeance. Felver wondered if McNair, who did not seem overburdened with a moral sense, hated Coper for what he did or for his station in life. If he hated Coper for being a member of the ruling class, then it would be easy to be indignant at his conduct also. Felver doubted that McNair would have similar contempt for Heid, who had observed the observer and then blackmailed him. Indeed, McNair had been quick to ask which one was low in Felver's judgment.

"So Heid squeezed him for it, and then took off, uh?"

McNair's face was still tense. "I'm not so sure he left town."

Felver tried to connect stray details and couldn't do it. Whether Heid had gone or stayed, why was McNair using his horse? Felver frowned and then asked, "Have you seen him?"

"Not since shortly after Coper got back."

Felver paused as he felt a chill go through him. Again he felt the prickly feeling in his head. "You think Coper did something to him?"

McNair blew smoke down toward his own chest. "He wouldn't dirty his hands."

Things clicked into place like the oiled cylinder of a six-shooter. Coper had come back, Hodges and Carter had struck camp, and Heid had dropped out of circulation. McNair at

232

some point had no doubt been an accomplice at least by being aware of the thefts and the blackmail, so he was vulnerable now, without Heid's support. Small wonder that he would be willing to spill the beans on Coper. Not only was he striking a blow at the high and mighty, but he was also making it possible for Coper to get locked up. The sooner the better, before Coper sent his thugs on another little job. Felver assumed that was what McNair had borrowed the horse for — to get out of town himself.

"Was it because Heid knew? If it was, why didn't Coper do it sooner?"

McNair's voice sounded matter-of-fact. "I think it was because Heid upped the ante."

Again, Felver had the sense that McNair did not disapprove of Heid's entrepreneurship in itself. As the stable man had said, they were thick. If McNair was willing to talk now, it was because at this point he couldn't hurt Heid by anything he said to expose Coper. Felver gave it another little push. "Seems like a dirty way to try to get out of it."

The fire came to McNair's eyes. "Damned dirty. It wouldn't hurt my feelings if he had to swing for it."

Felver found himself agreeing, even as he thought that blackmailing was rather low itself and might not be totally undeserving of consequences. He looked at McNair, whose sunken eyes glowed with resentment. Even if McNair had a different scale of ethics, he had one. At his own level, he apparently had a sense of justice and was getting even on Heid's behalf. Honor among thieves, as it was called, at least had its code.

"You don't know it for sure, though, do you?"

"No, but I've got a damned good hunch."

It seemed like a tight, desperate world at the moment. Felver thought McNair might even resent having benefited from Coper's patronage, to whatever degree he might have done so. Whatever the case, it seemed clear that McNair wanted to land a good blow before he made a run for it. Felver thought that somewhere in this murky world, perhaps for lack of someone closer in spirit, McNair placed a small degree of trust in Felver.

It was worth a try. He had nothing to lose by asking another question. "Where might a fellow look for evidence?"

McNair gazed at the floor as he exhaled smoke. "It wouldn't hurt to start by lookin' in the cellar of Coper's house."

Chapter Thirteen

As Felver rode back into town from the stock pens, he sifted through the impressions he had gained from McNair. Coper had been in thick with Hodges and Carter all along, even before Felver had come to town. When the two upstarts had come to his camp to try to run him off, they were probably working in Coper's interests. Coper might have taken alarm at Felver's comment about peeking through windows, not because Felver would have known anything but because Heid had been sitting there. Coper might have wanted to run him off before he could learn anything from Heid. Naturally, Coper would have wanted to push him away from getting to know the girl any better, as well.

He wondered where Hodges and Carter had gone to. Coper had probably paid them for their earlier work so he could get them to do one last job. Felver thought of them as what they were — low-class thieves and probably killers, out to make easy money and prove themselves. They probably had no idea of Coper's deep-down motives; if they had known why he needed more money and then had to do away with Heid, they would probably have sneered at him. Felver shrugged. They might have taken his money anyway.

It really was a lot of trouble that Coper put people through, just to cover up his own acts of guilt. Caught at something that ugly, he might have thought there was no other way out. For all his respectability, he had a mass of vile matter inside him, and he was probably desperate to keep it from view.

Felver thought about the links in the chain he had followed. His early hunches about Coper had been right, but he had had to find out in what way they had been right. It was like working his way through a series of rooms, and when he got to the innermost room, he was not surprised to see who was there. But he was surprised at why. Felver remembered a clever saying, that there was always one more sonofabitch than you counted on. He thought he had had them pretty well counted, and he had, but the saying still fit. Coper counted for two.

Felver had let his horse take a slow walk along the side street, and now he took a cross street. The center of town, what little there was, lay straight ahead. As he rode into the main street, he heard his name called.

Looking ahead, he saw Dalhart on a bay horse. Felver waved, and Dalhart came trotting over.

"Been lookin' for you," said Dalhart, as he slowed the bay and turned it.

"I was expecting to see you sooner, but when

I didn't, I decided to go ahead on my own."

Dalhart fell in alongside. "Well, we got off to a slow start, it bein' Sunday. Then Prunty, he come in with the news that he saw our young friends."

Felver looked across at Dalhart. "Is that right?"

"Uh-huh. They made a camp out at the Sexton breaks."

"Where's that?"

"South and west of the ranch."

Felver tried to place it. "Would that be near the line shack we built?"

"Farther west and a little north."

"Oh. Uh-huh. And what are they doin' there?"

"Prunty said it looked like they were layin' around gettin' drunk. He got a pair of field glasses and went back out to keep an eye on 'em, and I came in to look for you. Have you turned up anything?"

"I believe so." Felver looked around. They were in the middle of the street, in the middle of town. "Let's ride out a little ways, and I'll tell you."

Dalhart glanced around. "Which way?"

Felver twisted his mouth. He had already ridden back and forth between the stock pens and the livery stable, and he thought he had put in enough of an appearance in the main street. He didn't know the layout of the north part of town, but he had the impression that most of the houses were there. He motioned south with his head. "Let's go back this way and walk along the creek."

When they reached the creek, they dismounted and walked together. In a low voice, Felver summarized what he had heard from the bartender, the stable man, and McNair.

Dalhart gave a low whistle. "He's into it up to his neck."

"It sure sounds like it. It seems to me that what we need to do is round up all three of 'em as soon as we can."

"From what Prunty said, those other two are likely to be around for the rest of the day."

"Well, then, I suppose we go to the sheriff and try to close in on Coper first."

Dalhart led the way to the sheriff's office, which sat on the north side of the main street, across from the hotel. The door was locked, and no one answered to Dalhart's knocking, so he went around back. A few minutes later he returned.

"He's coming."

Felver glanced at the sun, which was still high but in the west. It was that time of day when a working man started to feel tired but knew he still had a couple of hours to go. The sun rays on the side of his face reminded him of that feeling.

Before long there came a rattle at the door. It opened inward, to show a man who looked as if he had just gotten up from a nap. He had disheveled reddish-brown hair and a thick mustache of matching color. He seemed still to be opening his wide, blue eyes. He looked to be in his late thirties, perhaps thickening at the hips. In his stocking feet, he was taller than Dalhart and Felver.

He introduced himself to Felver as Sheriff Chambers and told the two of them to come in. As he spoke, he showed a good set of teeth.

Dalhart and Felver sat in straight-backed, wooden chairs while the sheriff took a seat in a wooden armchair behind the desk. Dalhart introduced the topic, starting with the burglaries that the sheriff had investigated. Then Felver took over, telling the story very much as he had just told it to Dalhart.

The sheriff followed the story with interest. His eyes were wide and alert now, and he nodded from time to time to show comprehension. At the end of the story he drew a deep breath and said, "I don't have a deputy, but if you boys would like to go along, we can pay a visit to the Coper household."

The boys agreed, and the sheriff got up and padded out of the office. In a couple of minutes he was back, wearing boots, a hat, and a gunbelt.

The three of them walked down the sidewalk on the north side of the street, past the barbershop and the mercantile, both of which were closed now. At the corner before the block that held Five Star Drayage, the sheriff turned right and headed north. Two blocks later, after crossing the street, he turned left and crossed again.

"This is it," he said, nodding at the house on the corner.

Felver looked at the house. He had wondered which one was Coper's house, and now that he saw it, it looked rather common. It was a square house, facing south, with a small enclosed porch for an entry. It had a pyramid roof and a cement foundation. The yard was bare, with the exception of one small cedar tree on each side of the dirt walkway leading up to the steps.

Felver and Dalhart waited on the ground while the sheriff rapped with the door knocker. Felver's stomach was fluttering as a long moment dragged by. The sheriff knocked again and rested his hand on his pistol butt.

Felver heard a door open inside, and then the entry door opened. Mrs. Coper stood in the doorway.

"Good afternoon, Mrs. Coper," said the sheriff. "I'm sorry to bother you, but I'd like to speak with your husband if I could."

Mrs. Coper's eyes glanced down at the two men in the yard and then back up at the sheriff. "He's not here."

"Oh, I'm sorry for the trouble, then. Do you think he might be at his office?"

"I don't know where he is. He doesn't usually go to his office on Sundays."

Felver recalled seeing two of Coper's men making a delivery earlier in the day, but he said nothing.

The sheriff waited for a moment. Then, taking off his hat, he said, "I really am sorry for the bother, but I wonder if you might help us."

"It's not any bother, and I'd be glad to help if I could."

The sheriff lowered his hat to his left side. "Do you think we could take a look inside?"

"Do you mean to search the house?" Her beady eyes narrowed at the sheriff.

"Primarily the basement," he said. "Not your personal living quarters."

Mrs. Coper glanced at Felver and Dalhart.

"These two boys are my helpers," said the sheriff in an assuring tone. "They won't be any trouble."

"Come on in," said Mrs. Coper, turning to lead the way into the house.

The interior of the house was dark, as the shades were drawn. The sheriff paused just inside the front room, with his helpers behind him. "Could I trouble you for a lamp?" he asked.

"Of course. I'll be right back." Mrs. Coper moved away and disappeared in a dark hallway. A minute later she returned, with the glow of a kerosene lamp in front of her. "This way." Her voice sounded soft and ghostly.

She led them through the kitchen and stopped at a door. Her face, though pasty and pale, looked calm as she handed the lamp to the sheriff.

He took the lamp and put his hat back on his head. "Thank you. Now it seems as if we might need something else. A shovel."

"There's one down there," she said, still in her soft voice. "He had a couple of young men doing something down there last night, and I saw a shovel when I went to take a look this morning."

She's all right, Felver thought.

"Thank you, Mrs. Coper," said the sheriff. Raising the lamp, he opened the door and peered into the stairwell. Then his boot sounded as he stepped down.

Felver went next, with Dalhart behind him. The cellar had a musty smell of earth. Down on the floor, in the glow of the lamp, Felver could see it was a dirt cellar, not a paved basement. The foundation of the house sat back about five feet on all sides, so that the cellar was a pit with an earthen ledge all around it. As the house was not large, the cellar was even less so, and the stairs cut off some of the floor space.

"There's the shovel," said Felver, picking it out where it stood in the corner. He moved toward it and laid his hand on it.

The sheriff held up the lamp and moved it around. Felver saw a heap of wizened potatoes, a collapsed pumpkin, and a broken crate with burlap bags stuffed in it.

"Looks like someone has tromped down the dirt here," said Dalhart.

"Let's have a look." The sheriff moved the lamp to his left, and the arrangement of light and shadow moved with him.

Felver looked at the ground and could see boot-prints packed in close to one another, side by side, in rows. Touching the tip of the shovel to the dirt, he looked at the sheriff, whose face was half in shadow. When the sheriff nodded, Felver knew why he had been invited along. He made a shallow scrape and lifted the first shovelful of dirt.

Dalhart and the sheriff stood aside and let him do the digging. The dirt was soft and easy, even though it had been packed. Felver continued to make shallow cuts until he determined that the fill dirt was at least a foot deep. Then he dug out the first foot of dirt all the way around and determined the shape and length of the hole.

Not knowing which way the body lay, and not wanting to dig up the face first, he hunched down and dug deeper into the middle of the grave. At about a foot deeper, he felt the tip of the shovel hit something. He dug more lightly now, still taking dirt out of the middle. Whenever the blade of the shovel went a little deeper, he felt resistance and a slight give. He wasn't hitting wood; he knew that.

He scraped and scooped and lifted dirt, as much by feel as by sight. Half the hole was in shadow, so he beckoned for the sheriff to move the light forward. He wanted to see enough of the middle of the body to know which way it was lying. With better light he lifted more dirt, little by little, as he scraped with the shovel turned on edge. Finally he saw brown cloth, and he knew it was Heid's suit.

With a few more minutes of digging, he uncovered the waist and lower arms. Heid was lying with his feet toward the staircase. Felver scraped away more dirt, then used the tip of the shovel to shake dirt from the hands, arms, coat, and vest. Then he realized something was missing: Heid's watch and chain.

Felver let out a long breath. "He's laid out with his head this way," he said, motioning to his right. "Do you want me to dig him out the rest of the way?"

"Just the upper half for right now," the sheriff answered. "Enough to make an identification."

Felver took a deep breath and went back to his work. Knowing the depth, he took out the bulk of the dirt more quickly now. Then he scraped with lighter strokes until he had about an inch to go. What he wanted to avoid at any cost of extra effort was to strike Heid's face with the shovel, so when he had gone as far as he dared, he set the shovel aside. Reaching down and grabbing the dead man's wrists, he lifted the upper body in a slow pull. Dirt spilled off of the sides and into Heid's lap as his head and face, powdered with dirt, came into view.

Felver let the body sink back onto the dirt, some of which had slipped underneath and now gave Heid the appearance of lying propped up.

"No question about who it is," said the sheriff.

Felver stood up and back, wiping his hands on his pants. His mouth was dry, and he had a knot in his stomach. It was too bad, he thought. Heid had gotten himself into this trouble, but it still didn't seem fair.

Dalhart cleared his throat but said nothing.

"Well, that's good enough for right now," said the sheriff. "Why don't you boys go up first, so I can be the last one to leave the scene. Just a precaution, for when it goes to court."

Felver climbed up the stairs with Dalhart two steps behind. At the top of the stairway, Felver opened the door into the kitchen, where he was pleased to see lamplight. Farther on, he saw light in the front room as well.

Mrs. Coper came into the kitchen and laid a small, leather-bound book on the table. Bound with a clasp, it was the type that people used for keeping a diary. As the sheriff's footsteps were audible coming up the stairs, Mrs. Coper stood waiting until the sheriff stepped into the kitchen.

"Here," she said. "I think this is all that is left." She turned and walked out of the room.

The sheriff took the book and laid it on the table, then opened it. A recess had been cut out of the inside, to give it a hollow compartment. The sheriff lifted out the contents — half a dozen small photographs of young women. The pictures had been trimmed into circles and ovals and hearts, as such photographs were trimmed to fit into lockets and small gilded frames.

"These were probably taken out of the valuables," said the sheriff. He looked at Dalhart and Felver. "Do you recognize any of these?"

Felver shook his head. The young women looked innocent, and some of them pretty, but he did not know any of them.

Dalhart shook his head also. "The boss's girl isn't in there. But her picture might have been too big to fit in that book." Dalhart shook his head again. After looking around, he said in a lowered voice, "I can understand why he would take the pictures out, so the things wouldn't be identified so quick, but I wonder why he kept the pictures."

Felver looked up and away from the table. He thought it was one more way that Coper intruded on other's people's privacy. Letting out a breath, he said, "Just to look at, I guess."

Turning from the table, he saw again that a light was lit in the front room, so he headed in that direction. Dalhart followed.

"I'll be right there," said the sheriff, "as soon as I put these away."

As Felver reached the front room, he was

startled by a noise in the entryway. The door opened, and Felver saw a brown suit, a dark Vandyke beard, a pair of dark, close-set eyes, and dark hair pressed down to suggest that Coper had left his hat in the entryway. His eyes met Felver's in a cold stare.

"What are you doing here?"

Felver, catching motion to his left, saw Mrs. Coper approaching. His mouth was dry as he said, "Your wife let us in."

Coper's face took on a strict look as he turned to his wife. "Georgiana, what are these strange men doing in my house?"

Her pasty face and beady eyes showed nothing but calm as she said, "They asked if they could take a look, so I let them in."

The steady look on her face made sense to Felver. He remembered the first time he had seen her and had felt he had an incomplete impression of her. Now she seemed complete. She was nobody's fool.

Felver heard the sheriff's step behind him, and he saw Coper turn to look. The close-set eyes seemed to waver for a second until Coper's face firmed up.

"What's the matter?" he asked the sheriff.

"With your wife's permission, we did a little digging in the cellar. I think you know what we found."

Coper looked around at all four people and returned his gaze to the sheriff. "I can't say that I do. I had some men down there straightening up, and for all I know, they might have left something."

"They might have," answered the sheriff. "The good thing is, we know where to pick them up right away, so we can ask them."

Coper showed no emotion. "I hope you do."

"Meanwhile," said the sheriff, "I'm placing you under arrest for being accessory to murder."

The eyebrows lifted above the narrow eyes. "Whose murder?"

"You can go take a look in the cellar if you're sure you don't know."

"No, thanks. I don't care to look at dead people."

"Only live ones?" said Felver.

Coper turned to look at Felver. "What's that supposed to mean?"

"You know well enough," Felver answered.

"And then there's the matter of these pictures," said the sheriff, holding up the book. "As soon as we get some of them identified, I'll have another charge against you. For right now, a dead man in your cellar is enough for me to take you to jail." The sheriff turned. "Mrs. Coper, I'll send someone to take it out of there. Again, I'm sorry for the trouble."

Mrs. Coper gave a cool look at her husband and then said to the sheriff, "It's no trouble for me."

The sheriff took a pair of handcuffs from his vest pocket and said, "Let's put these on. Boys, you can wait outside."

Felver and Dalhart went out to stand in the yard. Long shadows stretched away from the houses in the neighborhood, and the sun was about to set. It was a calm evening, like the one before. Felver remembered sitting on the bench in front of the café and enjoying the simplicity of the evening. Perhaps as he sat there, or a little after, Heid's life had come to an end. It was too bad the young man couldn't have lived a straight life, but it was too late now. Everybody got one chance, and no one knew how long it was going to last. When it was over, the world went on. The sun would come up again the next day, and some people would do things straight as others hatched their crooked schemes.

Felver looked at Dalhart, who was rolling a cigarette. He imagined Dalhart had his own thoughts.

"A little rough going," said Felver.

Dalhart nodded. "Sorry I let you do all the diggin'. I'm just not very good at some of those things, so I was in no hurry to jump in."

"No matter," said Felver, shaking his head. "It's not so bad in comparison. Even if Heid was crooked, he probably deserved better than that."

Dalhart cleared his throat, but before he said anything the door opened. Coper stepped out with his hat on his head and his hands cuffed in front of him. The sheriff followed him down the steps and then fell in beside him. At the corner, the sheriff headed straight toward the main street, going back the way he had come but on the opposite side of the street. Felver and Dalhart followed a few paces behind. Dalhart smoked his cigarette as they walked. Nobody spoke.

They slowed as they came to the corner of the main street. As the sheriff and Coper turned left, Felver looked down the street to his right, where a horse stood in front of the office of Five Star Drayage. A shadowy figure rose up from behind the horse and made a motion, after which a crash of glass sounded. The dark figure jumped into the saddle, and the horse galloped away as the rider bounced in the seat. Felver was sure it was McNair. The man was wearing something other than a hat, and he bounced in the saddle like an inexperienced rider.

The sheriff and Coper both turned around in the direction of the noise. Felver and Dalhart ran down the sidewalk, with the sheriff and Coper close behind. Already a glow was appearing in the window, and smoke was edging out through the large hole in the glass.

"It's a fire!" Dalhart shouted.

Coper's voice sounded indignant. "The sonofabitch threw a firebomb! Unlock my hands."

"Hell, no. For all I know, that's why he did it." Then the sheriff called out in a sharp voice,

"You two boys, go after that bastard on the horse. We'll see to this."

Dalhart tossed his cigarette into the street as he and Felver took off running for their horses. "Who was it?" he asked.

"It looked like McNair," said Felver, between breaths.

The horses were a good three hundred yards away, so after the first fifty-yard sprint, Felver slowed to a trot. Dalhart caught up and ran even with him, the two of them clomping along in their boots. Voices were sounding along the street now.

"Fire!" hollered Dalhart. "Go help the sheriff!"

They came to the hitch rack, untied their horses, pulled their cinches, and were gone in an instant. The horses were on a dead run in less than a block. Smoke was starting to billow out of Five Star Drayage, and the sheriff was shouting orders from the sidewalk, where he stood with his hand on Coper's arm. Felver saw that much as he flashed by, and then his attention focused on the rider up ahead.

He was sure it was McNair, and he had to appreciate the timing. McNair must have been watching, waiting for the sheriff to come along with Coper in tow. It must have given him a bitter pleasure to know he had gotten Coper arrested and then to firebomb the place while Coper stood there with his hands tied.

Horse hooves drummed, and the ground

flowed away beneath Felver's eyes. McNair had started with a lead of about a mile, but Felver and Dalhart were closing the gap. Felver looked off to his left and could see the dull face of Red Bluff in the dusk, and below it, the white spot that was his tent. Looking ahead again, he could see the rider a half-mile in front, still bouncing.

He could tell something was wrong up ahead. The rider was bouncing to the left, and then on the side of the horse, and then on the ground. The horse slowed to a walk as the man got up, limped a few steps, picked up something, and put it on his head. He limped toward the horse, which looked back at him and then walked ahead, with its reins trailing out to the side.

Now that he actually saw McNair, Felver had less of a desire to catch him. In the excitement of the fire and the shouting, he had taken off on the chase without asking himself if it was really his place to do so. Now he slowed his horse to a stop, and Dalhart did the same.

"What's the matter?" asked Dalhart. "Do you think he's got a gun?"

"I'm not worried about that," said Felver. "But when it comes right down to it, I don't care if we catch him."

Dalhart jerked his head around. "Why?"

"I don't think he stole anything — not that he wouldn't — and I know he didn't kill anyone. The worst he did was know about it, and he helped us catch the big fish."

"I thought we were chasin' him because he set that fire."

"Oh, I guess we were. But they've probably got it out by now." Felver turned his horse and looked toward town, then at Dalhart as he said, "Don't you think?"

Dalhart looked in the direction, then up the trail where the figure was limping after the retreating horse, and then back toward town. "I guess so. I don't see any bonfire."

"Neither do I."

They turned and rode slowly back toward town.

"I don't know," said Felver, "but when we got that close, it didn't seem that important to catch him."

Darkness had settled in when they reached the main street. The smell of fire hung in the air, but no flames showed in the night. Felver and Dalhart rode to the sheriff's office and reported in.

"It's too bad you didn't catch him," said the sheriff. "I'd like to have held him for a while."

"He had a pretty good lead on us," Dalhart said, "and we didn't see any sense in breakin' our own necks in the dark."

"Well, to hell with him, then," said the sheriff. "We'll get those other two in the morning. You're sure they're not goin' anywhere?"

Dalhart laughed. "I don't think they're goin' anywhere, but I'll ride out and tell Prunty.

Then he won't let 'em go even if they try."

Back outside, Felver told Dalhart he would ride to the ranch in the morning and square up with the boss. Dalhart rode off, and Felver was left to himself. He walked past the café, but no light showed from the kitchen. Jenny would be in her room now, and it wouldn't do to go to the hotel and try to send for her. He would see her the next day.

He stepped into the street and looked up at the stars. It was too bad someone like Heid would never be able to see them again, but it was good that Coper had to look through bars if he was going to see them at all. Then there was McNair, out under the stars. He would have a long night of it, limping after a horse that would stay a few yards ahead of him. When he caught it, he would be all right for a while, and wherever he ended up next, he would have plenty to think about. Then, if not before, he might come to the conclusion that Heid had paid for him one last time, and he would probably understand why Felver gave up the chase.

Chapter Fourteen

As Felver rode out to Percy's ranch the next morning, an image of Coper's shameless face kept coming back to him. He had thought Hodges and Carter were brazen, but they were nothing in comparison with their master. Face-to-face with his wife and other witnesses who knew him for what he was, he had acted as if he had done no wrong and would be justified. Even before he walked out of his house, he must have had a sense of public exposure, at least for the thefts and murder. He must be feeling shame, even if he had no remorse for what he had done and all the trouble he had caused. To Felver, that seemed the capstone — to deny the shame.

Turning his thoughts forward, he had a mild feeling of misgiving or apology. He and Dalhart had been able to put a finger on the thieves, but they had not been able to recover any of the stolen items. What was gone was gone.

When Felver arrived at the ranch, he found Percy sitting at the mess table, drinking coffee. Sounds from the kitchen told of Clarence's whereabouts. Percy had a calm, resigned air about him as he invited Felver to sit down.

"Jim and Bill went on out to the breaks before sunup this morning. I imagine the sheriff's there by now."

Felver took off his hat as he sat down. "I'm sorry we didn't do any better."

Percy gave a wave of the hand. "There's nothing that can be done. As I figure it, that stuff was long gone when you and Jim first started looking for it."

"I believe so."

Percy went on. "It's just not right. You turn your back, and someone comes into your house, steals things that mean something to you, and then goes off and gives them to someone else to pawn."

"No, it's not right. Stealin's bad enough, and that makes it worse."

"I don't like the idea of that fellow having his hands on Mary Anne's picture. It's a good thing I kept out of it, or I wouldn't have been as nice as Bill was."

"Well, I know it won't get your stuff back, but at least someone will have to answer for it."

Clarence came with the coffeepot and a clean cup. He poured coffee for Felver, refilled the boss's cup, and went back to the kitchen.

Percy let out a breath. "I'm sorry for that boy that got killed, even if he had his finger in it somewhere. That's probably what'll hang these three, if anything. But I hope they get charged and sentenced for the stealing, too."

Felver thought of the other, unspoken wrongs that Coper had committed. "Yeh," he said, "it seems as if Heid paid more than he should have, and Coper won't have to pay enough. I'm sure the sheriff will charge him with theft, though."

Percy took a drink of coffee. "Well, I guess there's not much we can do about some things." He looked at Felver. "And I do appreciate your part in it. If you hadn't found out what you did, he might have gotten away with it."

An image of Coper's house flashed in Felver's mind. "Maybe. He might have been able to sit on it for a long time."

"Well, I appreciate what you did. The least I can do is pay your wages. It doesn't seem like much."

"Just four days. Seemed like a week, but that's all it was."

Percy paused for a moment before speaking. "Do you know what you're going to do next?"

Felver had an image of a girl in light-colored hair. "I think I'll just move along, like before."

The boss scratched his beard. "Do you need anything?"

Felver raised his eyebrows. "Actually, I do. I need a gentle riding horse. But I suppose I can find one."

Percy gave a puzzled look and then shrugged it away. "That might not be so hard. I've got an older horse that if you don't push him much, he's still got some work left in him."

Felver paused to give it some thought. "I

could take a look at him. Dependin' on what he's worth, my wages could pay for part of it."

The boss made a slow blink. "Well, look at him."

When they had finished their coffee, they put on their hats and went outside. Percy led the way to a fenced pasture in back of the ranch buildings. The pasture was about twenty acres, and it held a dozen horses grazing in the morning sunshine.

Percy pointed with his arm out straight. "It's that brown horse, third one from the right."

Felver looked at the horse, which stood a couple of hundred yards away. It was a medium-sized horse, a little heavy — probably from not being worked much. Its back had begun to sway, but the animal did not look broken down.

"Do you want to ride him? He's been rode plenty, but not since roundup. We used him for a night-herdin' horse."

Felver nodded. "If he moves around all right, that should be good enough. I can take your word that he's gentle to ride."

"That he is." The boss pushed down a strand of wire to climb through the fence. "Let's go in, then, and move 'em around."

The two men climbed through the fence and went on a fast walk toward the horses. The brown horse stood and looked until they came within fifty yards, and then he picked up his feet and trotted away.

"Well, he's not lame," said Felver. He had already decided that if the horse gave any trouble at all, he could ride it and let Jenny ride his. "I think he'll do."

"Well, good enough, then."

Felver looked at the horse, which had run another fifty yards out and then stopped. "How much is he worth?"

"Oh, hell, just take him. We'll call it square on the wages."

Felver looked at the boss. "Seems a little uneven."

Percy shook his head. "I don't use him much, and I couldn't get much for him if I tried to sell him. This way, I'll feel good about it." He gave Felver a square look. "I mean it."

"Well, thanks." Felver looked again at the horse. "I suppose I should go get my own horse and rope this one out."

The two men went back to the ranch house, and the boss went inside. He was no doubt used to letting men do their work. Felver led his saddle horse to the pasture gate, slipped inside, and mounted up. Within a few minutes he had the brown horse on the end of his rope. The horse did not fight at all but fell right into place. He looked like he was about fifteen years old and had seen plenty of work, but his feet still worked.

Back at the ranch house, Felver saw two riders coming in from the southwest. It looked like Dalhart and Prunty. After a couple of minutes he could distinguish Prunty's flat-brimmed brown hat from Dalhart's tall-crowned gray hat, and as the horses turned he recognized Prunty's lean frame.

Felver waited until they rode into the yard. Dalhart was all smiles, with his teeth flashing, but Prunty looked glum as usual. As the two riders swung down from their horses and tied them up, Felver saw that they were both wearing six-guns. Prunty gave a nod and went into the bunkhouse.

"Well, we got 'em shipped," said Dalhart.

Felver laughed. "That's good. Did they give you any trouble?"

Dalhart took a deep breath and let it out. "Well, they looked like they wanted to break camp this morning, but we talked 'em out of it. Then, for good measure, Prunty tied 'em up together, and in a moment of solemn truth, I couldn't say that he didn't slap 'em around a little to get the lashes good and tight."

"But the sheriff's got 'em now, uh?"

"Oh, yeah. He came out with a couple of other boys, and they're probably halfway back to town by now." Dalhart glanced at the brown horse. "Are you tradin' horses?"

"The boss made me a deal on this one. I think I'll be headin' on down the trail, and I thought I could use another horse."

Dalhart glanced again at the horse. "Well, he's not a colt anymore, but you'll get some use out of him." Dalhart looked back at Felver.

"Well, I guess there's not much to keep you here, but whenever you're back this way, be sure to drop in."

"I will. And it's been good to know you."

They shook hands, and Felver went inside to say good-bye to the rest. Prunty mumbled a good-bye, and Clarence said good-bye and good luck. Percy thanked him again and told him to come back when he got a chance, especially if he didn't have anything to do around fall roundup time. Felver said he would keep that in mind.

Back outside, he saw Dalhart leaning against the hitching rail and smoking a cigarette.

Dalhart gave him a broad smile, as if he had figured something out. "So long, Felver. And good luck."

"Thanks. And so long."

Felver untied his two horses, climbed into the saddle, and straightened out his rope. He waved to Dalhart and rode out of the yard.

On his way back into town, Felver realized he was hungry. Now that he thought of it, he hadn't eaten since yesterday noon. It was his own fault for not getting to the ranch sooner or staying longer, but he had had other things on his mind. Now he was hungry. The sun was reaching straight up, so he thought he would get to town in good time for dinner.

He was plenty hungry by the time he rode into the main street. Life seemed to have picked up as usual on a Monday, as there were wagons in the street and horses at the hitching rails. As he passed Five Star Drayage on his left, he saw the broken window and the charred interior. The fire had not spread much, but it had been good for a flourish.

He tied the horses in front of the café and went in to eat. He gave his order to Nell the waitress, drank coffee until his meal came, and then did his best not to rush the pleasure. When he was finished, he asked Nell to tell Jenny that he would be back after the dinner hour. Then he paid Mr. Garth and went out for a shave and a bath.

As he soaked in the tub, he thought about Jenny. He remembered the doubts he had had, and he was pretty sure they were gone. She seemed a good match for him, the same kind of person. He remembered thinking that he could make a decent woman out of her, but now he knew it wasn't a matter of lifting her up. She had been there all along, and it had just taken him a while to see it. Now it seemed as if it was the two of them, side by side, seeing if they could put together a decent life. Although the last few days had indeed seemed like a week, he had seen her just the morning before, and their understanding had been clear. They would leave together as soon as they could get things arranged.

When he returned after being gone an hour and a half, the café was almost empty. As he sat down, Nell caught his glance and went into the kitchen. When Jenny came out, Felver could tell he had the right feeling.

"What do you know?" he asked as she approached his table.

She smiled. "As opposed to what do I think?"

"Well, what do you think, then?"

"About what?"

"I don't know. What about that brown horse standing outside without any saddle?"

She craned her neck up and looked toward the window. "I don't know. It looks like a horse."

He smiled up at her. "Do you think you can ride him?"

She shrugged. "I guess so. A saddle would help."

"I'll try to find one this afternoon. And then he's yours to ride."

Her blue eyes flashed. "Really?"

"Really," he said. He put his hand on the table, and she put hers on top of it. He smiled up at her again and said, "Can you take a minute and step outside with me?"

She gave a slight frown. "Well, yes."

Out on the sidewalk, he helped her step down into the street, into the open air and sunlight. Standing by the brown horse, he said, "I didn't want to ask this in there where somebody might hear me." He took her right hand in his left. "Other than finding a saddle and packing up my camp, I'm ready to go. I just wanted to be sure I wasn't out of line assumin' that you still want to go with me."

"Of course I want to," she said, squeezing his hand.

"I think we can give it a decent try." He looked into her shining blue eyes. They were moist, and he could feel that his were, as well.

"I think so, too," she said.

"Well, then, how long do you think it would take you to get things in order?"

Her eyes sparkled. "I think I could draw my pay and get checked out of my room tonight, if you wanted to come back for me."

"Sure," he said, thinking he had been almost too quick to answer. "We probably wouldn't get started until the morning."

"That would be all right."

He took her other hand and drew her close, then kissed her under the open sky, not caring if the town still had an eye. Standing back, he smiled and said, "We can get a good night's rest."

She smiled and nodded, and he thought of her words. Things were going to be all right.

W